Knight's Castle

Knight's Castle

Edward Eager

ILLUSTRATED BY
N. M. BODECKER

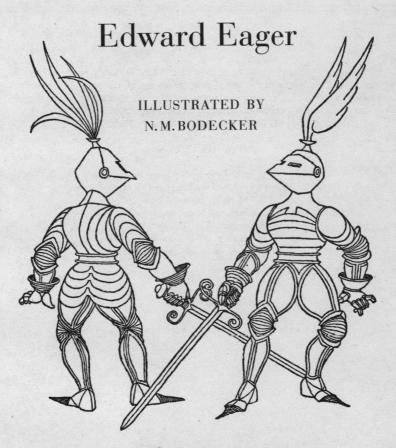

SCHOLASTIC INC.

New York Toronto London Auckland Sydney
Mexico City New Delhi Hong Kong Buenos Aires

ISBN 0-439-32226-X

Copyright © 1956 by Harcourt, Inc.
Copyright renewed 1984 by Jane Eager and N. M. Bodecker.
All rights reserved.
Published by Scholastic Inc., 555 Broadway, New York, NY 10012,
by arrangement with Harcourt, Inc.
SCHOLASTIC and associated logos are trademarks and/or
registered trademarks of Scholastic Inc.

12 11 10 9 8 7 6 5   2 3 4 5 6/0

Printed in the U.S.A.   40

First Scholastic printing, September 2001

For my son
FRITZ,
friend of knights
and castles

CONTENTS

1

The Blow

It happened just the other day, to a boy named Roger.

Most of it happened to his sister Ann, too, but she was a girl and didn't count, or at least that's what Roger thought, or at least he thought that in the beginning.

Part of it happened to his cousins Jack and Eliza, too, but they didn't come into it till later.

Roger and Ann lived with their mother and father in a pleasant small house in a pleasant small city, and until the blow fell life was very pleasant.

Their father was an understanding parent, often quite helpful and willing about such important things as building a rabbit hutch in the backyard or hanging the swing from the biggest oak tree. And even though he said he wasn't good with his hands (which was true), still part of the rabbit hutch stayed together quite nicely (though all the rabbits got away through the part that didn't), and one year the swing didn't fall down till nearly the end of summer.

And best of all, their father always read to them for an hour after dinner, even though they'd been able to read perfectly well to themselves for years now. This practice sometimes led to hot argument, because Roger was getting to be rather a yeomanly type and wanted to hear books like *The White Company* and *The Scottish Chiefs*, while Ann was becoming all too womanly, and leaned toward *Little Women* and the Betsy-Tacy books. And their father would complicate matters by always wanting to read books like *Five Children and It*, which he said was great literature. And Ann agreed that, next to the Betsy-Tacy books, it was.

Roger enjoyed science fiction books, too, but there their father drew the line. He said they were like having bad dreams on purpose, and if the Flying Saucers really *have* landed, he didn't want to know about it. Roger called this Not Taking a Realistic Attitude. All the same, he really liked the magic books his father and Ann loved so, and back in the days when he was a child, before he got to be eleven, he had even hoped that some day something magic would happen to *him*. But nothing ever had, and that seemed to Roger to prove that there was no such thing. Or if there ever had been, probably modern science had done away with it long ago.

Their father always said how could he be sure, and besides, even if there weren't any such thing as magic, wasn't it pleasant to think that there might be? And in the discussion that would follow, their mother would sometimes pass through the room and cry out, and say honestly, their father was as much of a child as *they* were, which Ann thought quite a compliment, though she was not sure their mother meant it as one.

Ann was eight, and believed nearly everything.

When their mother wasn't passing through the room and crying out, she was quite an understanding parent, too, except about the way Roger kept wanting more model soldiers when he had two hundred and fifty-six already, and the way all two hundred and fifty-six were always to be found all over the floor of his room, which she said passed all understanding.

And sometimes when Roger would start picking on Ann because she was a girl, and younger, their mother would get really cross, and say there would be none of that in *this* house! Their mother said she knew just how Ann felt because *she* had been a girl once, too, and the youngest of *four* children, and what she had endured worms wouldn't believe!

But at other times she talked about what fun she and her sisters and brother had had; so Roger decided she couldn't have suffered so very much. And when he asked his Uncle Mark about it, his Uncle Mark said their mother had been a terror to cats and ruled the household with a rod of iron. And when he asked his Aunt Katharine, his Aunt Katharine said their mother had been a dear little baby, but went through a difficult phase as she grew older. He couldn't ask his Aunt Jane, because she was hardly ever there, being usually occupied hunting big game in darkest Africa or touring the English countryside on a bicycle.

But he decided their mother's childhood had probably been very much like their own, partly good and partly bad, but mostly very good indeed.

And so time went on, with few clouds to stir life's untroubled sea, until the day the blow fell.

The blow fell on a day in June. School had been over for only a few days, and the whole bright vacation lay ahead, waiting for them to make up their minds where to spend it. Their mother wanted to tour New England and stop at all the antique shops looking for old spice boxes, which she liked for some reason, and their father wanted to revisit an island in Canada, where he'd spent a wonderful summer once, back when the world was young.

Roger wanted to go somewhere yeomanly, like Sherwood Forest, but since everybody else seemed to think that was a bit far, he decided the Rocky Mountains were the next best thing. Ann didn't know where she wanted to go yet, but she thought probably Wampler's Lake, to be near her best friend Edith Timson. They were to have a big family conference about it that evening and decide.

But that afternoon their father came home from the office at half past three instead of half past five, and he didn't explain why, but said hello to Roger and Ann, just as though everything were perfectly usual, only somehow he didn't sound as though everything were.

And a few minutes later he and their mother

went into the living room and shut the door, and their voices went on and on, for what seemed like practically forever.

Roger and Ann didn't know what to think of this odd behavior, but then they got interested in seeing who could draw the most horrible Frankenstein monster, and forgot about it. And after they'd drawn, and compared, and argued about which was most truly horrifying, Roger tried to persuade Ann to join him in a war of model soldiers. Only Ann was never terribly interested in model soldiers; so they played *Monopoly* instead.

But after a few minutes of this, Ann got to thinking about that door being closed, though she didn't say anything about it to Roger. And after a few minutes more, Roger found himself wondering about those voices going on and on, though he didn't say anything about it to Ann.

And five minutes later all subterfuge failed, and they looked at each other and nodded with one accord, and put their *Monopoly* game away (which was unusual of them) and went and stood on the stairway. The living room door was still closed, and from where they stood they could hear only an occasional unrevealing word, but the voices sounded serious.

"I sense divorce in the air," said Roger, who

had been seeing too many old movies on television lately.

Ann shook her head. "They don't sound angry, just kind of worried. Do you suppose Father's done something *criminal*?" (Ann had been seeing old movies on television, too.)

"Not Father," said Roger. "He's too nice and not half crafty enough. The police would catch him right away."

"Maybe they *have*," said Ann. But it turned out neither guess was right.

For the voices stopped and the door opened at last, as voices and doors will, and their mother and father came out, and looked at them with false bright smiles, and said it was time for dinner. And dinner was their mother's specially good meat loaf and popovers, but somehow the two children couldn't enjoy any of it, and every popover was as lead.

Finally Roger put his fourth popover down on his plate half-eaten, and burst into speech. "It's not fair," he said. "It's not fair, not telling us what's the matter, when anybody could see something *is*!"

"We're not babies," Ann chimed in. "We can stand it, no matter how terrible."

"It's not terrible," their father said. "Only I'm afraid we won't get to the Rocky Mountains this summer, or Wampler's Lake, either."

And then he said he guessed he'd go and serve the dessert, and while he was out of the room their mother told them.

She told them their father had something wrong inside, and he was going to have to go to a hospital in Baltimore, Maryland, to have it made well. And because she didn't want to be separated from their father at a time like this, their mother was going to Baltimore, Maryland, too. And because it was all going to cost a lot of money, they wouldn't be able to send the children somewhere else for their vacation, and so she and Roger and Ann were going to have to spend the next few weeks in Baltimore, Maryland, and no one could tell how many weeks it would be, but maybe it would be the whole summer.

"Your father hopes you won't be too disappointed about the mountains and the lake," she finished.

Roger didn't say anything for a minute. Then he got red. Then he said, "It isn't that. It's Father."

"I know," said their mother.

"Is it serious?" said Roger.

"Doctor Reese is almost certain he'll be all right," said their mother.

"Almost," said Roger.

"I know," said their mother.

Ann didn't say anything. But when their father came in a second later with the dessert, which happened to be Royal Anne cherries and sponge cake, she ran to take the tray from him, as though its weight might be too much for his feeble strength.

And Roger jumped up and pulled their father's chair out for him, as though he might not be able to manage it alone.

And when they took their places at the table again, Ann didn't eat, but sat looking at their father with an expression on her face that Roger would have called icky if he hadn't had a sneaking suspicion that he was looking the same way himself.

Their father ate two Royal Anne cherries. Then he looked up and saw Roger and Ann. He swallowed hard, as if he were swallowing a pit in one of the cherries. Then he grinned.

"Look, kids," he said. "We may as well get this straight. I don't have a pain, and I'm not weak and pining away and having to be waited on. I've just got something mixed up inside that has to be straightened out, and we're going where the doctors are who can do that best. And we won't any of us have time to worry, because we've got to leave in three days and it'll take all that time to get ready."

After that, Roger and Ann found that their dessert went down more easily, though neither of them was ever able to feel quite the same about sponge cake or Royal Ann cherries again. Still, if their father could be brave, who were they to be behind-hand?

Their mother was making plans. "Maybe we can stay with your Aunt Katharine while your father's in the hospital," she was saying.

"No, Martha," said their father. "We can't go wishing ourselves on people, like that."

"I don't know why not," said their mother. "My own sister. That beautiful big house."

"Even so," said their father, two words which were law in that house.

"I'll call her, anyway," said their mother. "Maybe she can find us an inexpensive hotel."

Ann and Roger looked at each other. The words didn't sound very promising, suggesting mean chandeliers with light bulbs that were too small, and long dark corridors and a draught coming in under the door. Still, this was no time for selfishness; so they volunteered to do the dinner dishes, and tried to cheer each other with bright conversation. Once Ann said, "Poor Father," and Roger said, "Yes," and once Roger said, "You forgot to scour the sink," and Ann said she was just going to.

When they came out of the kitchen their mother was just hanging up the telephone. "She insisted,

Fred. I just knew she would," she was saying. "Children, we *are* staying with Aunt Katharine after all. Now you'll have Jack and Eliza to play with."

"Oh," said Roger. Ann threw him an understanding look.

"Oh what?" said their mother.

"Nothing," said Roger. And then it was time for Ann to go to bed, and Roger to go upstairs for a half hour of tapering off before his own bedtime.

"Jack and Eliza!" muttered Ann to Roger, on the stairs. "Help!"

Up till two years ago their cousins Jack and Eliza had lived in the same town they did. The last they'd seen of Eliza she'd been just about the bossiest nine-year-old girl on her, or any other, block. As for Jack, all he cared about was his Leica camera, and spent all his time in his darkroom, only coming out for meals, or, as Ann once said wittily, to cast his shadow, like Groundhog Day.

"He's pretty good at baseball, though," said Roger.

"That," said Ann, "is small comfort."

"Ann, go to bed," said her mother, from below; so she did. But once there, she lay awake wondering about Baltimore, Maryland. All the words made her think of was a Baltimore oriole. She tried to picture a city all orange and black, like an oriole's feathers.

After a bit she tiptoed over to the bookcase and found *The American Family Encyclopedia*, Volume One, A—Boon. Baltimore, Maryland, she read, was the eighth largest city in the United States, population 859,100. Chief industries, iron and steel, straw hats, et cetera.

She got back into bed and shut her eyes, seeing a sky flaming with the orange of many steel forges, while in the black iron foundries below 859,100 dark figures labored, all wearing straw hats. "Only I should think the straw hats 'd catch fire," she murmured to herself. A second later she was asleep.

In his room, Roger sat on the floor among the two hundred and fifty-six model soldiers, and absently started a small war. He wouldn't have done it if anyone had been looking, of course. Now that he was eleven, he kept the soldiers just as a collection. But when he felt lonely or unhappy, or when things went wrong, he sometimes still secretly played with them, for all the world as though he were still only ten-and-a-half.

Two hundred and seven of Roger's soldiers were modern ones, British grenadiers and such, that he had bought himself, or been given. Thirty-one were World War One veterans that had belonged to his father, and seventeen were survivors of the Spanish-

American War, and of many a nursery battle since the days of Roger's grandfather.

The two hundred and fifty-sixth soldier was much older, even, than any of these. No one knew exactly where it had come from in the first place, but Roger's father said it had been in his family for generations. No one could tell what kind of soldier it was, or even if it was a soldier at all, because all its paint was worn off, and its weapon, if any, had disappeared in the sands of time.

But it was the size of a model soldier, and Roger and his father before him, and *his* father before *him*, had played with it along with their own soldiers, though each one's father had said it was an antique and shouldn't be handled.

Roger called it the old one, and usually gave it special duties like being a sentinel or scout, so that it wouldn't be damaged in the heat of battle. Roger's battles (particularly when he felt lonely or unhappy) were usually very heated indeed.

But tonight even the familiar call to arms wasn't much comfort. There was a small skirmish, and several gallant privates bit the dust, but Roger's heart wasn't really in it, and after a minute or two he got into bed and put out the light. And if he took one of the soldiers to bed with him I hope you will not scorn him too much. A model soldier is not the same thing as a teddy bear at all. Taking a model soldier to bed with you is much more mature, and more manly, too.

It was the old one Roger held in his hand, and as he lay thinking about the weeks ahead in Baltimore, Maryland, he clutched it hard. Of course if their father were going to be all right, that was the main thing. But he wished something fun and exciting could happen to him in Baltimore, Maryland, too.

Just as he was thinking this thought, a voice spoke. It wasn't the voice of conscience, either. It seemed to come from somewhere very near Roger, and it seemed both cross and sleepy.

"A murrain!" it seemed to say. "Just as I was beginning to feel rested! Ah well, back into the fray, a soldier's lot is not a happy one, a plague on it! Still, needs must when duty calls! I could not love sleep half so much loved I not honor more!"

Roger sat up in bed. His hand tickled. For a second he could have sworn the old one was stirring in his grasp, stretching and yawning. Roger opened his hand quickly, and the old one fell to the floor by the side of the bed, landing in a standing position.

"Rough play, by the rood!" he seemed to say. A moonbeam shining through the window struck a silver glint from his battered countenance, and for a moment he seemed to be turning to the other soldiers lined up on the floor, as though giving them a word of command. And then for another moment it seemed as though all the soldiers were moving in the soft light, marching toward Roger.

Roger rubbed his eyes and opened them again. The soldiers were still now. Nothing had happened. Naturally.

"I must be sleepier than I thought," Roger said to himself. "I'm seeing things that aren't there." And he plumped up his pillow and put his head down on it and went to sleep.

2

The Beginning

The next three days were a flurry of activity and packing and meeting each other on the stairs at odd hours with armfuls of clothes. And of course the children would forget, sometimes for half days at a time, why they were going to Baltimore, Maryland, and just be happy and excited to be going anywhere.

Roger's packing took the longest. First he dumped the whole contents of his clothes basket and his dresser drawers into his suitcase, and that was quick,

and the suitcase closed quite easily after he sat
it for a while, and he didn't actually have to *stand*
on it at all, hardly.

But then came the problem of choosing exactly
the right-sized grocery carton from the pile in the
attic, and then each of the two hundred and fifty-
six soldiers had to be wrapped carefully in cotton
and fitted into the box, not to mention sundry can-
non, tanks, drawbridges, turrets from old broken
castles, and other art treasures without which no
boy's life can be truly rich and full.

Their mother went so far as to suggest that there
were probably plenty of things to play with at Aunt
Katharine's without taking toys along, but one glance
at Roger's expression told her what a barbarous idea
this was.

And quite soon the night of the third day came,
and they were on the train. Roger and Ann had
traveled in Pullman cars before, and there was nothing about this particular Pullman car to distinguish
it from those they had known and loved in the past,
except its name, which was Wah-Wah-Tay-See. Ann,
who was making a collection of the names of Pullman
cars, wrote this down on a special page in her notebook.

Their mother and father had a drawing room,
and the two children were in the section nearest to

it, Ann in the lower berth and Roger in the upper. And the dining car menu, like all menus in trains, had tonight's dinner listed in the middle, and then around the edges lots of far more interesting dishes that apparently no one was supposed to order, because their waiter looked very surprised when Ann asked for pickled mangoes and Roger called for a bottle of Apollinaris water. The children's mother tried to thwart them in this project, but their father gave her his well-known let-them-do-it-this-once look, and she subsided.

When they got back to their car after dinner, the usual nice old lady turned up in the section opposite, and wanted to talk to them about a dear little fairy who lived in a Pullman car. Roger and Ann were polite about this, and luckily it didn't go on for very long, because the train was getting into Baltimore, Maryland, early in the morning; so bedtime had to be early tonight.

And when Roger, in his pajamas, hung his head down over the edge of the berth and poked it through the green curtains to talk to Ann in the berth below, the usual cross other old lady in the upper berth next door rapped on the wall and said, "Quiet!"

So after that Roger lay still and tried to go to sleep, but he couldn't. Ann, down below, could look out on barns and towns and moonlight and hotdog stands, but he had only a curving wall and curtains and the dim light from the corridor to gaze at.

Pretty soon he decided he couldn't stand gazing at them any longer. He opened his curtains, let his feet down over the edge, swung wildly in space, and thumped to the floor.

He looked in on Ann. A gentle snore issued from under a mound of blankets. So then he knelt on the floor of the corridor and felt under the lower berth till he found the grocery carton of soldiers. He'd take a few of the top ones out and have a war in his berth, that's what he'd do.

To get the string off the box was but the work of a moment, but wasn't so noiseless a process as Roger would have chosen, and just as he had his hand inside the top flap, the cross old lady in the upper berth next door parted her curtains and glared down at him with a face so truly horrible that all Roger could do was gasp, grab the first soldier he found, shove the carton back, scramble up to his own berth and pull the curtains. He lay clutching the soldier, his heart beating fast, waiting for the old lady to call the conductor or pull the emergency cord and stop the train. But nothing of the kind happened.

What did happen was that he felt a tickling in his hand again, like the time before, and when he turned on the little light with his other hand he saw that what he held was the old one and he was talking.

"Newfangled flummery!" he was saying. "Modern inventions, industrial revolution, rush, rush, rush, choo-choo, crash, bang! A castle that stayed put was good enough for me, aye, and my forefathers before me, and when we sallied forth 'twas a gallant steed under us, aye, and a trusty sword in hand! By my halidom!" he added.

"What did you say?" said Roger.

"Thou heardst me," said the old one.

"I did not," said Roger. "You didn't say any of that. You didn't talk that other time, either. It was a dream. So's this."

The old one reached out his small metal hand and pinched Roger hard. For such a small pinch it hurt quite a lot.

"Ow," said Roger. And then he knew. And remembering from his reading that Psammeads and Phoenixes and Mary Poppins always had to be addressed with due deference, he made his voice very respectful indeed.

"Oh Old One," he said, "I take it back. I see it all now. You *are* magic."

"Light dawneth," said the Old One.

"Why," said Roger, getting excited, "I suppose you must be the lucky charm of this family, like the

Mouldiwarp of the House of Arden! Only I suppose you've been handed down from generation to generation till people forgot you were magic and just used you to play soldiers with! I'm sorry if we played too rough. And those times I forgot to pick you up and stepped on you afterwards by mistake. I hope the magic hasn't all gone out of you. It hasn't, has it? Did you come to make Father get well in Baltimore, Maryland? Because if I get a wish, that's what I wish."

The Old One said nothing, but Roger thought he grew a bit warmer in his hand. Encouraged, he went on.

"And if you still have any magic left in you after that, I wish we'd have an adventure in Baltimore, Maryland, while we're waiting."

"Quiet!" said the voice of the old lady next door. And she gave a really terrible rap on the partition at Roger's feet.

So Roger put out his light, and placed the Old One carefully on the pillow next to him, where the dim glow from the corridor could shine on his face. And just before he went to sleep, Roger heard the Old One speak again.

"Gadzooks!" he said. "Cannot a man retire in his old age but paltry striplings must be waking him from his soft sleep with their wearisome wishes?

Wishes must be earned, sirrah! However," he added, and his voice was kinder, "wishes, like fishes, turneth up in strange dishes. Tomorrow is another day I always say." After that he was silent, and Roger knew somehow that he would not speak again, at least not now.

The next thing Roger knew, it was morning and his mother was telling him to wake up. And for the half hour after that all was bustle and squeak as he and Ann hurried to brush their teeth, hurried to pack away their pajamas and put on their clothes, and hurried to the dining car for breakfast.

Their mother had not been pleased to find the carton of soldiers untied, but she had already tied it up again, with a few pertinent remarks; so Roger put the Old One in his pocket.

And then the porter was brushing them off and they were pulling into Baltimore, Maryland, and Ann looked out of the window to see a city not orange and black, but gray with rain.

Their Aunt Katharine met them in the station. Eliza was with her, wearing her hair in pigtails and talking a blue streak. Jack was not to be seen, but a moment later the children caught a back view of him. He had his camera well in hand, and was focusing on some rather uninteresting-looking murals on the station ceiling.

"Wouldn't you know?" whispered Roger to Ann.

And then Aunt Katharine was kissing them and kissing their mother and shaking hands with their father, and Jack drifted up and took a picture of the whole group, and Eliza circled round all of them, telling all about a man she had heard of who had gone to the same hospital Roger's father was going to, and had practically *everything* taken out, and learned to walk again perfectly well after a year.

"Really, Eliza," said Aunt Katharine, which was all she ever said when Eliza was awful.

And now a smartly dressed chauffeur had appeared and was dealing with the luggage, and Aunt Katharine turned to the children's mother. "You'll want to go to the hospital right away; so I thought I could take the children to a movie and lunch and then meet you at the house." And this was agreeable to all.

There was a bad moment when Roger and Ann said good-bye to their father, for a thought that didn't bear thinking couldn't help flashing through both their minds. But their father grinned and said, "I'll be seeing you," and after that they felt better. And their mother and father rode off in Aunt Katharine's big black car, while Jack summoned a taxi in rather a grown-up fashion, and the others got in.

On the way uptown Roger and Ann hung out

the window looking for points of interest, but there weren't any till the cab stopped for a traffic light near a large statue. Ann read the name on the statue, *George Peabody*. She caught Roger's eye and they both started giggling, for no reason at all, as sometimes happens in families. To their surprise, Eliza giggled, too.

"George Cornbody," said Roger.

"George Squashbody," said Ann.

"George Beanbody," said Eliza. "George Applebody, George Prunebody."

Jack didn't say anything. He was leaning out the window of the cab, taking a picture of the statue. But after that Roger and Ann and Eliza felt friendlier, the way you do when you've all giggled at the same thing.

"Really, Eliza," said Aunt Katharine. "What movie shall we see?"

Jack and Eliza started talking at once. Jack wanted to see a picture about wheat growing that was full of interesting camera angles while Eliza was loud in asserting that *Scarface Returns* was absolutely the only decent thing in town.

Aunt Katharine shook her head. "I thought *Ivanhoe*," she said. Roger's eyes glowed, for his father had read him the book last year. And everyone else had to admit that *Ivanhoe* sounded just dandy.

And it was. It was in glorious Technicolor, and it was just about as yeomanly as a movie could be. Roger and Ann sat enthralled, and so, surprisingly enough, did Aunt Katharine. Jack quite approved of the photography, and as for Eliza, during the final combat between Ivanhoe and the wicked Knight Templar she bounced up and down in her seat and muttered, "Pow! Zowie! Wham!" till everybody sitting around said, "Shush," and Aunt Katharine said, "Really, Eliza."

But after the picture, as they sat eating a late and filling lunch of strange and wonderful seafood, Jack became critical.

"The tournament wasn't quite right," he said. "That isn't the way they did it, really."

"Were you ever *in* one?" said Aunt Katharine, turning suddenly on her son.

"No," said Jack, surprised.

"Then don't talk about what you don't know about," said his mother. "*I* thought it was quite a nice little tournament. Not like the ones King Arthur used to have, of course."

"Honestly, Mother," said Eliza. "Anybody'd think you'd been alive back then!"

Aunt Katharine blushed, and if you have read a book called *Half Magic* you will know why. But all she said was, "Who wants what for dessert?"

And there were seventeen things to choose from (because Roger counted), and that took silent concentration from everyone.

But a few minutes later Eliza looked up from her hot butterscotch ice-cream shortcake. "I don't see why he had to marry that old Rowena," she said. "Rebecca was lots prettier. Why couldn't he have married her?"

"That wasn't what the author wrote," said Roger, a bit shocked.

"Oh, that old Sir Walter Scott!" cried Eliza. "A lot he knew about anything!"

"Sir Walter Scott?" said Ann. "We have him in our *Authors* game."

"You don't still play *Authors*, do you?" said Eliza. "That's almost as babyish as *Old Maid*!"

After that Ann didn't feel so friendly about Eliza. Deciding not to talk, she got out her notebook, and started a new page headed, "Interesting Things About Baltimore, Maryland."

"Good movies. Good lunches. Statue of George Peabody," she wrote, and that seemed to be all the interesting things, so far. And then it was time to pay the bill.

As they rode to Aunt Katharine's house in another taxi, they passed a toyshop window, and Roger had an unworthy thought. He had hoped Aunt Katharine would give him and Ann presents; she usually did when she saw them. Still, they had had the movie and lunch, hadn't they? Roger decided his thought was *very* unworthy and should be suppressed.

Their mother was waiting for them at Aunt Katharine's, and told them everything was fine with their father so far. And then Aunt Katharine took them to see their rooms. "You'll have the whole east wing to yourselves," she said.

"My," said Ann. "We shall be in the lap of luxury."

And they very nearly were. There was a big bedroom for their mother, with her own bath, and a smaller bedroom for Ann, and another bath, and another big room that would be Roger's room and a playroom combined.

And when Roger and Ann saw this room, they stood and stared.

There was a big, fancy dollhouse, with a family of dolls, in one corner, and in another was an immense castle, the most wonderful castle Roger had ever seen, rich with turrets and battlements and a portcullis and a pretend moat, and a keep with a front wall that swung out on a hinge, so you could see what was going on inside. The dollhouse and the castle were from Aunt Katharine.

"Only I told her what to get," said Eliza, proudly. "Except not the dollhouse. I despise dolls, don't you?"

So of course Ann, who didn't, had to pretend that she did, only not loud enough for Aunt Katharine to hear and have her feelings hurt.

And their Uncle Mark in New York City had sent a big box of model soldiers, but these weren't like any Roger had ever seen before. They were from a wonderful shop called The Knight's Castle, and there were no two alike. There were knights of all sorts with beards of divers colors, and some young ones with no beards at all. There were squires and pages and bowmen in Lincoln green, and a few obvious dastardly villains and half a dozen ladies of high degree. Ann was sure one of the bowmen in green was Robin Hood and Roger found a stalwart, handsome young knight that everyone agreed could be only Wilfred of Ivanhoe.

There was still another present, from Aunt Jane, sent all the way from London by air mail.

"Isn't that just like Jane?" said Aunt Katharine to their mother. "So dashing and extravagant." Aunt Jane was in London for the Coronation, of course.

Wherever there was the most going on, Aunt Jane usually was. "Eliza is just like her," their Aunt Katharine added in a low voice, but Ann heard her.

Aunt Jane's package, when opened, proved to contain a lot of little books in blue covers. Eliza pushed in ahead of the others, to see what they were. "*The Magic City* by E. Nesbit," she said, in tones of scorn. "I read that *ages* ago! Magic is baby stuff."

Roger opened his mouth to agree with her. Then he remembered last night. His hand went into his pocket and encountered the Old One, still lying there. He proceeded with caution. "I know what you mean," he said. "Of course there might be a *little* something to it, though."

Eliza uttered a contemptuous snort.

And then the children's mother went downstairs with Aunt Katharine to have a good talk, and the children were left to play with the castle.

Only they couldn't get at the castle right now, because Jack was there before them, putting different knights in position in the different rooms and then taking their pictures.

Roger's fingers itched to get the knights out of Jack's hands. You could tell from the way he was setting them up that he didn't know a thing about the laws of chivalry. He just didn't have the touch. But after all, he was the host and Roger was the guest and had to be polite.

Eliza had no such scruples. "Get out of the way," she said, and pushed in next to her brother.

After that Roger decided it was free for all, and knelt down by the castle, jostling Eliza on one side and Jack on the other.

Ann would have liked to play quietly with her dollhouse in its corner but after what Eliza had said she didn't dare; so she joined the group around the castle.

"Let's have it be the one in *Ivanhoe*," said Eliza. "The one where the siege was."

"You mean Torquilstone?" said Roger, feeling rather superior.

"Whatever its name was," said Eliza.

So it was decided that the castle was to be that ill-starred fortress where the villains Bois-Guilbert and De Bracy held Ivanhoe and most of the other characters prisoner during the most exciting part of the story.

Luckily one of the knights had a Templar's shield; so he could be Bois-Guilbert, and Roger found a thin, overdressed one for De Bracy. Ann chose the darkest and most beautiful of the ladies to be Rebecca, and Eliza picked a simpering inferior-looking blonde for Rowena. Jack took pictures of the different characters.

There was a jester in the assortment, to be the jester Wamba, and an elderly knight made a fine Cedric the Saxon, Ivanhoe's father.

"Only he wouldn't be wearing just armor, silly," said Eliza. While Ann watched in alarm, she found some manicure scissors and went over to the dollhouse, and quickly made Cedric a scarlet cloak from the train of the ballgown of the mother doll, trimmed with fur cut from the same lady's fur coat.

The afternoon passed quickly and happily, save for a few moments when the strong personalities of Eliza and Roger met and clashed. By the time dinnertime came, the castle presented a spectacular appearance.

Bois-Guilbert was on the battlements pleading with Rebecca to give him her love and Rebecca was threatening to throw herself over the edge to the courtyard below. De Bracy was in a rich chamber of the castle pleading with Rowena to give him her love and Rowena was looking self-righteous.

Cedric the Saxon was in the dungeon with Wamba the jester beside him. Wilfred of Ivanhoe languished wounded in an upper room, his middle tied up in a bandage Eliza had made out of a dollhouse kitchen curtain.

A few stray knights, henchmen of the two villains, lounged about the castle courtyard, and at a safe distance outside on the greensward (carpet), Robin Hood and the Black Knight (a knight in black armor, naturally), with Maid Marian, who *would* come along (Eliza chose the most athletic-looking of the ladies), lay in ambush with a band of trusty archers, waiting to attack the castle. Eliza made the ambush out of some fluffy green stuff from the dollhouse bath mat.

Jack thought they ought to have the wicked Prince John, too, and found a bearded knight with a crown and a squint who looked the part. There wasn't any logical place in the castle for him, and he belonged in another part of the story anyway; so Jack pushed back the sliding wrought-iron screen of the fireplace, and the space within made an excellent throne room. Jack put a few stray knights in there with him, for courtiers. An armchair from the dollhouse made an imposing throne.

Anybody left over was an attendant. Halfway through arranging these, Roger remembered his precious soldiers from home, still packed in their cotton. But then he decided their uniforms wouldn't go with the armor of the others, and besides, now that he had the castle full of knights, the charm of British grenadiers and Spanish War veterans paled. So he left them in their box on top of the bureau.

But he did take the Old One out of his pocket, and put him in the castle, among the attendants, just in case.

And then, just as it was the moment for the Black Knight and Robin Hood and their followers to begin attacking the castle, Aunt Katharine appeared in the doorway and said, "All right, time to wash your hands and faces for dinner."

There really couldn't have been a worse time for her to say this, and Eliza let her know it. "Honestly!" she fumed. "You'd think mothers just waited outside the door till they're *sure* it's the wrong moment! We can't possibly come now; we're having a siege!"

"Really, Eliza," said Aunt Katharine. And then Eliza's father, who was Uncle John, appeared firmly in the doorway, and that was that.

Dinner was good, and the children had one small glass of wine each, which was interesting, but made Ann yawn all through her pecan pie until her mother said they had had a long day and Ann should go to bed now, but Roger could stay up and play for half an hour more.

"Good," said Eliza. "Let's have the siege."

Ann sent Roger a beseeching look.

"No," he said, nobly. "It wouldn't be fair without Ann."

"Let's have it, anyway," said Eliza, not nobly at all. But her father gave her a stern look and she subsided. And good nights were said, and five minutes later Roger sat on the floor of his room, to the sound of toothbrush noises from the bathroom, and gloated over the castle, and thought about the things he would do with it and the things that would happen in it, and pretty soon his head began to feel heavy, and he got up without being called, and went into the bathroom and brushed his teeth and put on his pajamas, and came out again and called good night to Ann, and climbed into bed.

He turned his light off, but the light from the hall (that Ann had asked to have left on) sent a golden glow into the room. It was a hot night, and pretty soon Roger pushed the bedclothes off, so that some of them slid down to the floor. The last thing he saw before sleep came was the castle, glimmering goldenly at him from across the room.

When he woke up the golden glow was gone and it was daylight. Right away he looked across the room, for the castle. Then he stared.

The castle was there, all right, but it seemed hundreds of times bigger, and yet at the same time it seemed hundreds of times farther away. And then

Roger looked down, and he saw that he wasn't in his room at all. He was lying on a great plateau of white rock, and there must have been a landslide recently, for there was a fall of rock and rubble to one side, leading down to the grassy plain below. And then suddenly he remembered the Old One, and then he knew. This was the adventure he had asked for, and magic was happening to him at last.

He waited a minute to see what would happen next, and nothing did, and the castle stood there, its turrets gleaming at him in the bright sunlight, and it was plain to Roger that the first thing to do was get over there near it.

He started picking his way along the fall of rock, which seemed to be the only way down from the plateau. The rocks hurt his bare feet, and he wished the magic had been thoughtful enough to provide shoes. The way got steeper as he went along, and he slid the last half of it, skinning one knee.

No bones were broken, however, and he got to his feet and began the long walk across the flat greensward toward the castle. He felt rather conspicuous and a bit chilly in just his summer pajamas with the short trousers, and he felt rather small, too, as he drew near the castle's lofty walls and saw how *very* lofty they were. Either the castle had grown to life size or he had shrunk to the height a toy soldier would be if he were eleven years old, and it didn't really matter which, because it came to the same thing in the end.

He began walking slower. He didn't exactly want to turn around and run, but he didn't exactly want to go on, either. At last he stood at the edge of the moat, looking up at the parapets, far above him. The castle presented a grim aspect. The drawbridge was up and the portcullis was down. The moat had real water in it now, and the water looked deep and cold. Roger shivered.

"So this is Torquilstone," he said aloud, trying to sound jaunty, "and I'm at the siege of it."

He wondered if he were meant to venture inside the castle, or if he hadn't better go find Robin Hood's attacking party instead. Yes, he decided, that would be much the safer plan.

But when he looked around for the besiegers, no living soul was in sight. He must remember to tell Eliza she was a good ambush-maker, when he got back. If he ever did.

At this moment a voice broke in on his thoughts. The voice came from a window slit in the watch-tower next to the drawbridge.

"Halt, paltry knave," said the voice.

"I *am* halted," said Roger. "Paltry knave yourself," he added, but he didn't add it very loud. The window slit was too narrow for him to see the face of the gatekeeper, but he could tell from his voice that he wouldn't like him at all. He sounded, in fact, like a foul churl.

"Stand where ye are," the churlish voice went on. "Come ye on aught of business with my lords, or mean ye mischief to us and ourn?"

"No, I'm just looking," said Roger. "Now I'll be going."

He turned to go. An arrow whistled past his ear, and then another. There was nothing for him to hide behind and if he ran he would be a perfect target; so he did the only thing he could think of. He fell flat on the greensward and shut his eyes.

Behind him he heard a creaking sound that could only be the drawbridge being lowered, a sight that doubtless would have been very interesting at some other time, only not now. Then came a sound of mailed boots on stone, and a foot spurned Roger where he lay.

There is nothing like being spurned by a mailed foot to make a person stop being frightened and start being angry instead. Roger sat up and glared around him indignantly.

Three men in armor stood looking down at him.

"What witless wight art thou," said one of them, "that cometh a-knocking at our door all half-naked of a morning?" He took Roger by the ear and pulled him to his feet.

"Ow," said Roger.

"Nay, 'tis a mere boy!" said another of the men.

"'Tis a sign! 'Tis witchcraft!" cried the third, in alarm. "A changeling boy out of Elfland left on our doorstep in his shift, pardie! What can it mean?"

"Don't be so superstitious, Lionel," said the first man. "More likely some scurvy Saxon trick. Be ye Saxon or Norman, boy? Parlez-vous français?"

"Non," said Roger, in one of the two French words he knew.

"Aha! What did I tell you? A Saxon spy!" cried the first man. "Quick! Hail him before our masters!"

And Roger was seized and trundled across the drawbridge and through the outer courtyard and into the great hall of the castle keep. Two of the men hurried off in different directions to fetch their masters, and the third man, Lionel, was left on guard.

Now that the worst seemed to be happening, Roger began to feel more cheerful, and even a bit reckless. After all, every magic adventure he'd ever read had turned out fine for the hero in the end. I do not know how he came to be so sure that he was the hero of this one, but he was. It is simply a thing that one knows, and if you have ever been the hero of an adventure yourself, you will understand.

He stood looking about the great hall interestedly. It was just about as yeomanly as a hall could be, what with trophies on the wall, deerskins on the floor, and a whole boar roasting merrily on a spit in the great fireplace.

Then he looked at Lionel. Lionel smiled nervously and backed away a few paces, and this gave Roger an idea. He decided to have some fun with the superstitious guard. He went on looking at him for a minute, and then suddenly he made a terrible face and uttered a sepulchral cry.

"Beware!" he cried.

Lionel jumped. "What didst thou say?"

"Woe!" Roger went on, pleased with the success of his efforts. "Wurra wurra. Pity the poor Normans on a day like this!"

Lionel was looking pale. "Wherefore sayest thou such?" he asked. "Whence camest thou hither?"

"Wouldn't you like to know?" said Roger, forgetting to sound like a grim oracle and sounding like a mere boy. Then he recollected himself and started over. "Ask not the dread name of whence I came," he said, "but hearken to my dire words.

This day bringeth doom to all Normans within this castle!"

"Oh, dear," said Lionel. "Doth it really? What shall I do to be saved?"

"Flee," said Roger.

Lionel turned, and started to flee. But at that moment Brian de Bois-Guilbert and Maurice De Bracy entered the hall.

Both knights were thoroughly out of sorts, because they had both just been interrupted in important love scenes, and both their ladies had just rejected their proposals. Bois-Guilbert in particular was in a vile mood. He stalked up to Roger and stood glaring down at him.

Roger began feeling less reckless. It is one thing to play with a toy castle and wish you were back in the golden days of chivalry, and it is another thing to be really there, and have one of the greatest villians in all legend stand glaring down at you and breathing the hot breath of wrath in your direction.

Bois-Guilbert went on glaring for what seemed like ages. Then he said, "So!"

"Hello," said Roger, trying to smile in an offhand manner.

"Silence," said Bois-Guilbert. "I perceive that thou art a vile spy. Thou shalt hang from the castle battlements for the crows to pick at, as a warning to all Saxons!"

"Nay!" cried Maurice De Bracy, ever the less evil of the two villians. " 'Tis too harsh a punishment. He is but a child."

"He is no child," gibbered Lionel, excitedly, "but an elfish spirit come to warn us of disaster!"

"Tush, Lionel," said De Bracy. "What old wives' tale is this?"

"Take note of his garb, sir!" Lionel went on, almost in tears and pointing to Roger's summer pajamas. "Saw ye ever the like of that on mortal boy? Nay, but be sure the small fiends dress so, down below, what with the hot climate and all!" Fearfully his hand shot out and caught Roger by the collar of his pajama jacket. He saw the label inside the collar, and recoiled. "B. V. D.!" he read, in tones of horror. "Meaneth not that 'Bene volens diabolus,' or 'Best wishes from the devil?' "

"Pish, Lionel," said De Bracy. "Thy Latin waxeth rusty." But his voice sounded a bit worried, all the same.

Bois-Guilbert was made of sterner stuff.

"Go to," he said. "Never yet did Brian de Bois-Guilbert quail before witch or warlock. I defy the foul fiend. And besides, I don't believe it, anyway.

Kneel, minion." And he pushed Roger rudely to his knees before him. "Confess who hath sent ye hither and from what Saxon pigpen ye hail!"

"Nobody sent me. I came of my own accord," said Roger. "From Baltimore, Maryland."

"I know no merrie land save England," said De Bracy. "And la belle Normandie, of course."

"Quiet!" said Bois-Guilbert. "Who conducteth this inquiry, anyway? Minion," he said again to Roger, "for the last time I bid ye speak. What is your errand here?" And he, too, spurned Roger with his mailed foot.

Once again the spark of anger glowed in the soul of Roger. "All right," he said, in words more spunky than yeomanly. "All right! I came to help the good guys beat the bad guys! And that means *you*!"

Bois-Guilbert burst into unpleasant laughter. "And didst think a Templar's cheek would pale before a minikin *your* size?" he cried. "Away with him to the dungeon for the rats to nibble till he is ready to speak the truth!"

Maybe it was the mention of the rats that did it. Because if Roger had thought twice, he'd have gone quietly to the dungeon and bided his time, and let the story go on from there, and the ending might have been very different. There might have been a fair jailer's daughter to set him free, or there might have been a secret passage from the dungeon, or the rats might have proved friendly, and nibbled his bonds instead of him.

But which of these fascinating things would have happened will never be known, for Roger didn't think twice. He lost his temper instead, which is a dangerous thing to lose when you are in the middle of a magic adventure.

"Your time is up, Templar!" he cried. "Might as well throw in the sponge now! Wilfred of Ivanhoe beats you in the end, anyway, you know!"

"Ha!" cried Bois-Guilbert. "So *he* is thy master, is he?" He spat elegantly into a corner. "*That* for Wilfred of Ivanhoe! Knowest thou not he fell wounded at the end of the tournament and none hath seen him since? Where's your Wilfred of Ivanhoe now? Dead, that's where!"

"A lot you know about it!" said Roger, throwing precaution to the winds. "He's lying wounded right here in this castle now!"

"Oh, he is, is he?" said Bois-Guilbert, interestedly.

"Yes, he is," said Roger. "Rebecca's been taking care of him."

"Oh, she hath, hath she?" said Bois-Guilbert.

"Yes, and then when the castle catches fire he gets rescued," said Roger.

"Oh, the castle catcheth fire, doth it?" said Bois-Guilbert.

"Yes, and you know what? Robin Hood and his band are waiting outside right now, getting ready to besiege you, and guess who's with them? The Black Knight, that's who! Only do you know who it really is? It's King Richard, back from the Crusades, in disguise!" Roger finished triumphantly.

"Oh, it is, is it?" said Bois-Guilbert.

"Yes, it is," said Roger.

"One thing more," said Bois-Guilbert. "About this fire in the castle. Where doth it start?"

"Well," said Roger, "in the book it starts in the fuel magazine, but in the movie it starts in the dungeon."

"I know not this word movie," said Bois-Guilbert, "but just to be on the safe side . . . Guards, ho!" he suddenly called.

Men in armor started pouring into the room from all sides, and it was then that Roger realized, too late, what he had done. He had been overconfident. He had been boastful and too full of himself, and he had given the whole show away, and betrayed Ivanhoe and his friends into the hands of their enemies! Even so, he couldn't understand it. This wasn't the way the story went, at all!

"Form bucket brigades!" Bois-Guilbert was saying. "Some in the dungeon and some in the fuel magazine. Observe fire prevention rules. Watch out for flying sparks! Put out any flame thou seest!"

Some of the guards scurried off to do his bidding.

"You can't do that; it's not in the book!" cried Roger, running up to Bois-Guilbert.

"What is this talk of books?" said the Templar. "Out of my way!" He gave Roger a push to one side, and turned to some of the others. "Fetch me hither the wounded knight Rebecca hath been tending," he said grimly. "Stay not to be over-gentle with him, neither!"

"I didn't mean it! I take it back! It isn't him!" Roger cried, forgetting all grammar and running up on Bois-Guilbert's other side, to pummel at him vainly, as high up as he could reach.

But already more guards had hurried away to fetch Ivanhoe, and Bois-Guilbert, shaking Roger off, turned to the rest of his followers. "To arms!" he cried. "Enemies are without! A scurvy outlaw band led by him who calleth himself the Black Knight. But we shall be ready for them. Hugo, prepare the molten lead. De Bracy, wave a white pennon from the parapet and ask for parley. When the Black Knight steppeth upon the drawbridge, Hugo, empty thy caldron."

"What, and kill the king?" said De Bracy.

"Oh, no," said Roger.

"Prince John will thank us for it," said the Templar. "Besides, how were we to know who he was? People who goeth about in disguise can just take the consequences. The molten lead will make him unrecognizable, anyway."

"I'll have no part in it," said Maurice De Bracy.

"Good for you," said Roger.

"Oh, very well," said Bois-Guilbert. "Do I have to do everything myself around here?" And he turned and started for the courtyard.

Roger, made brave by guilt and fear, ran to bar the way. "Treason! Murder! Help!" he cried.

The Templar looked down at him with a face of utter exasperation. "Really!" he said. "Will no one cage this bratling for me?"

Ready hands seized Roger and dragged him back, and for a moment he decided he was going to end up in the dungeon with the rats after all. But there was an interruption.

The guards who had been sent to fetch Ivanhoe returned, carrying that gallant knight, still wounded and palely loitering upon a litter. They set the litter down, and Rebecca rushed in after them and flung herself on her knees beside him. A moment later

Rowena rushed in, pushed Rebecca out of the way, and flung herself on *her* knees where Rebecca had been.

Bois-Guilbert stood looking at his enemy with a cruel smile. "So we meet again," he said, "and for the last time, I think. Thou shalt rue the day thou unhorsed Bois-Guilbert in the field! But ere I finish *thee*, thou shalt see the end of that Lion-heart king thou servest. Guards, up with him and after me!" And once more he turned and strode through the courtyard.

The nearest guards lifted Ivanhoe and bore him after the Templar, and the whole multitude hurried along after *them*, curious to see the fine sport. Roger broke away from his captor and ran along with the others, and if a tear stained his cheek as he thought of the disaster he had brought upon those he had come to help I do not think you will blame him.

Suddenly, to his surprise, a friendly hand caught hold of his, and he looked up to see Rebecca, running along beside him and smiling at him with her kind sad eyes.

"Weep ye for Richard and Ivanhoe, boy?" she said. "Weep not. Fortune may yet change."

"Don't," said Roger, pulling his hand away and feeling guiltier than ever. "You wouldn't if you knew."

The people ran through the courtyard and up

the stairs till they gained the roof. Then they stood in sudden hush. Bois-Guilbert was already at the parapet, waving his white pennon of truce and calling for colloquy with the Black Knight, and down below the Black Knight, tall and noble, was coming forward for the supposed parley. The drawbridge had been lowered and the Black Knight was just stepping upon it, and up above, crouched behind his battlement, the villainous Hugo was just tilting his horrid, steaming caldron.

And it was then that Roger knew what he had to do. He lowered his head, butted his way through the crowd, and with a mighty effort hoisted himself up onto the battlements, between Hugo and Bois-Guilbert. He leaned from its dizzy heights and called, "Chiggers! Look out below! Cheezit!"

The Black Knight looked up. "Who saith so?"

"Me. Roger," was all Roger could think of to say. But it was enough. The Black Knight jumped back just in time, and the molten lead splashed hotly and harmlessly upon the empty stones below.

And then the men of Robin Hood, furious at the trick that had been played, leaped into action and the siege of Torquilstone began. A green-clad archer appeared from behind every bush and tree, and arrows fell like deadly rain.

The followers of Bois-Guilbert, caught all unprepared on the castle roof, made a fine target, and many fell under that first flight of arrows.

And now Robin's men ran up nearer the castle, and their bows twanged again, and the noise of their battle cries echoed round the walls of Torquilstone. And while they should have been calling, "À Robin, à Robin," or possibly "À Richard, à Richard," it seemed to Roger that they were saying, "À Roger, à Roger!"

Wilfred of Ivanhoe, though still pale, had leaped from his litter, seized a sword from a varlet standing near him, cleaved the varlet in half, and was now cutting a swath through the men of Torquilstone, taking them all on singlehanded, while Rebecca helped him by tripping up any who would attack him from the rear, and Rowena helped him by turning away and holding her ears.

Only Brian de Bois-Guilbert took no part in the battle that raged within and without the castle. He stood glaring at Roger, where he still clung to his lofty parapet.

"Witch-brat!" he said viciously. "Thou shalt learn what it meaneth to thwart me, when thy brains lie dashed out on the stones below!" And he seized Roger by a foot to thrust him over and down.

Roger looked down at the stones and didn't like what he saw. Then he looked at Bois-Guilbert and liked him even less. Then, just as all hope failed, he remembered something.

"I'm not afraid of you!" he cried. "You're not even real! You wouldn't even *be* Bois-Guilbert, if I hadn't said you were! You're nothing but a lead soldier!"

"What?" cried Bois-Guilbert, his face deathly pale and his voice a mere whisper. "What didst thou say?"

"Lead soldier!" Roger repeated wildly. "That's all any of you are! Lead soldiers, lead soldiers, lead soldiers!"

Bois-Guilbert fell back shuddering before him, and the fighting men dropped their swords and all the people fell on their knees, and a murmur of awe ran from lip to lip among the crowd.

"The Words of Power!" cried some, and "The Elfish Charm!" cried others, and "I said 'twas no mortal boy!" cried Lionel.

And Roger jumped down from his perch and pushed his way through them, and as he did so they seemed to grow paler and dimmer, and as he ran down the stairs the walls of the castle seemed to grow fainter, the way the picture on your television set does when a tube is ailing and your mother has to send for the man.

In the courtyard a figure with a white beard

appeared in Roger's path. Roger didn't recognize him but he seemed to recognize Roger, and to shake his head at him rather sorrowfully as he ran past. And yet just before everything faded out completely there seemed to be a twinkle in the figure's dim eye.

And now the castle had vanished and the sound of battle had died away, and all around and before Roger was nothing but gray mist. Then suddenly the plateau loomed whitely in his path as he ran, and he had just strength enough to scramble up the rock path to the top before darkness overtook him and he knew no more.

The next thing he *did* know, it was still dark, and he was sitting up in bed, and his mother was standing over him. "Did you have a bad dream?" she said. "You pushed the covers all off onto the floor."

"Yes," said Roger, sleepily, "I had a dream. Some of it was bad. Some of it wasn't, though. Anyway, it's over." And he rolled over and went back to sleep.

But it wasn't over.

The Magic City

When Roger woke up for the second time it was morning, and the castle was its normal self again, and yet he remembered it all too clearly when it hadn't been. And looking back on his behavior in the cold light of morning, he decided it could only be called un-yeomanly!

Of course there had been that one stirring moment when he saved the Black Knight's life, and the air rang with shouts of "À Roger, à Roger!" He guessed lots of people he knew would call a moment like that the high point of their whole lives.

But on the other hand the Black Knight's life wouldn't have needed saving if Roger hadn't given him away in the first place. And then at the end what did he do but run away without waiting to see who won the siege?

He wondered whether he would ever have a second chance, or if the whole thing was a mere failure. And it was as he was lying there wondering that Ann came bouncing into the room and sat on the bed (and on part of Roger) and said, "Let's play. Let's play with the castle."

"Go away. It's too early. I'm asleep," said Roger.

Eliza appeared in the doorway in her pajamas and bathrobe. "Let's play with the castle," she said.

"He says he's asleep," said Ann.

"I'll fix that," said Eliza. She laid hold of Roger and pulled. Roger kicked out. A small table bit the dust and several knees were skinned.

Jack appeared in the doorway. "What's the matter?" he asked.

"It's Roger," said Ann, from the sidelines. "He won't play with the castle."

"Oh. Well, I guess it's his castle," said Jack. He went out again.

Roger got up from the floor, got back into bed, and pulled the covers over his head. They came out at the foot. His bare toes emerged, and he could not feel that he made a dignified picture. He sat up again.

Eliza was staring at his bare feet with an expression of disdain. "It's not fair," she said. "Here we've been waiting all night to start playing with the castle, and you've been in here in the thick of it, just *glutting* yourself with it till you're tired of it!"

"That's not it," said Roger.

"What is, then?" said Eliza.

Roger didn't answer. The two girls sniffed, put their noses in the air, and went out arm in arm.

Breakfast was no better. Ann and Eliza made private jokes and giggled together. They did not address Roger. Roger felt depressed.

He wished he could ask them to play with the castle, but he couldn't. Now that he had known the knights in all their lifelike glory, just merely playing with them didn't seem possible. It would be a mockery.

Not only that, but there was the wish he had made about his father's getting well in Baltimore, Maryland. The Old One had said wishes had to be earned, and Roger felt that his behavior last night could not have done his father one bit of good.

But after breakfast their mother took them to see their father, and he didn't seem a bit worse, and they stayed for lunch and Roger was cheered. And when they got back to Aunt Katharine's, Jack asked him if he wanted to see some pictures being developed, and it was surprising how interesting photography turned out to be.

Ann heard Roger laughing in the darkroom, and was encouraged. She opened the door. "*Now* can we play with the castle?"

Roger turned on her with a face of fury. "*Now* see what you've done!" he said. "You've ruined the negatives. *Never* open the door of a darkroom!"

It was Ann's turn to feel depressed. She wandered upstairs to Roger's room. Eliza was curled up on the bed, reading *The Magic City*. "I'd forgotten what a good book this is," she said.

"I tried it," said Ann, "but the words were too big." She sat down on a chair, feeling lonely. Eliza glanced at her.

"Oh, all right," she said, in a long-suffering voice. "I suppose I'll have to start over, and read it to you."

"*Would* you?" said Ann, in surprise. Really, she thought, Eliza could be quite nice, once you were used to her. Her bark was worse than her bite. And she read out loud beautifully, putting in all the expression.

The Magic City proved to be all about a boy named Philip, who built a town of blocks and books and ornaments and peopled it with all his toys, and then one night the town came to life, and Philip found himself in the middle of it, and the magic adventures began.

"This," said Ann, after chapter one, "is a good book."

"This," she said, after chapter two, "is one of the crowned masterpieces of literature which have advanced civilization."

Eliza put the book down. She looked from the book to the castle in a significant manner. "What are we waiting for?" she said.

Ann looked shocked. "We couldn't. What about Roger?"

"He won't mind. It won't be *playing* with it at all, exactly. We won't even *touch* the castle, hardly. We'll detour round it, sort of. He'll never even know."

"Well," said Ann, hesitating.

Half an hour later Jack and Roger came into the room. Roger was whistling a merry tune that broke off in the middle as he stopped and stared.

The castle was still there and the dollhouse was still there and Prince John still held court in the fireplace. But all around and between and among them, the room was littered with books and ashtrays and tumblers turned upside down till it looked as though someone were holding a rummage sale on the floor. And down on the carpet, amid the coffee cups and boxes and perfume bottles sat Ann and Eliza, with two pairs of manicure scissors, busily cutting roses out of the flowered quilt from the dollhouse master bedroom and gluing them onto wooden matchsticks.

"What are you doing?" said Roger.

"Making a magic city," said Ann, happily, balancing one of the matchsticks upright on the carpet and sticking it there with some Scotch tape. "This is the rose garden."

"Well, you can just unmake it again," said Roger.

It was then that the mild and agreeable nature of Ann suffered a change. She got up and threw the scissors down on the floor. "I hate you," she said. "You're mean. And spoilsport and doggish in the manger!"

Jack looked at the city. "What's wrong with it?" he said, reasonably.

Roger looked at it, too. A sidewalk of stone

blocks led away from the castle, flanked by a double row of glittering columns that ended suddenly where the supply of old ginger ale bottles had given out. There was an imposing building made of books, labeled "Public Library," and another beautiful one made of different-colored cakes of soap, labeled "Public Baths." And since you can always find more drinking glasses and glass ashtrays and perfume bottles than you can anything else when you're building a magic city, the whole area sparkled with transparent domes and pinnacles.

"It's too modern," Roger said. "All that glass. It looks all streamlined. It isn't yeomanly. Castles didn't have sidewalks."

"This one does," said Ann.

"It's a good city. If you like that kind of thing," said Jack, looking down on it from his superior height of twelve-and-a-half years. "I vote it stays." And he went out of the room.

"Majority rules," said Eliza. "Three out of four."

"But it's all changed around and everything's spoiled!" Roger burst out desperately. "It just isn't Torquilstone any more! I hoped maybe I'd have a second chance, and now I *know* it won't happen again, and I never will!"

"Never will what?" said Eliza.

"Nothing," said Roger.

"Come on, Ann," said Eliza. "Let's go finish our book someplace else. He's crazy. Let him tear the old city down if he wants to."

"No, it's all right," Roger said. "Let it stay."

"Well, it won't be any fun unless we all do it together," said Ann. And she started out of the room after Eliza.

Roger had a change of heart. Ann was right; things *were* more fun when you did them together. "Wait," he started to say. But a closing door was his only answer.

The rest of Roger's day is better left untold. Let other pens dwell on guilt and misery. Suffice it to say that night came at last, and another day dawned, as usual, and Roger woke up with the sun in his eyes. He looked across at the castle. The castle looked back at him, small and toylike. Not a thing had happened. The magic was over. He had had his chance and he had failed.

Then suddenly as he looked he remembered the old man with the white beard he had met in the castle. And he went over and found the Old One and held him in his hand.

"Oh Old One," he said, "what's wrong? Is it the mistakes I made or is it because Ann built the city?"

To his joy he felt the familiar sensation of the

Old One growing warm in his hand, and the tiny, leaden voice began to speak.

"Ods bodikins!" said the Old One. "Hath it come to this? Hath the race sunk so low that all useful knowledge is forgotten, by the mass? Modern education, psychoanalysis, nuclear physics, a pox on it! What booteth thy newfangled fads and fancies if thou forgettest the good old rule that magic goeth by threes?"

"Do you mean . . ." began Roger.

"Canst count, sirrah? Didst thou think magic hath naught else to do but be waiting on thee hand and foot, day in, day out, maybe yes, maybe no, whenever it please thy puling fancy? Think thyself lucky if it smile on thee one night in three!"

"The third night's tomorrow," said Roger.

"Grand news," said the Old One.

There was a silence. Roger waited. Then he said, "Is there anything else? That I ought to know?"

The Old One was already growing colder in his hand, but his voice came again, only fainter.

"And didst think thou couldst do it all alone, selfish? Rode ever knight on gallant quest without his gentle lady to speed him on and hark to his tale and tell him how he should have done it differently? 'Oh woman, in our hour of ease uncertain, coy and hard to please, when pain and anguish wring the brow a ministering angel thou,' as the poet saith. A trusty friend may oft prove helpful, too. Not to speak of cousins."

"Oh," said Roger. "Yes. I see what you mean."

"Then act upon it," said the voice, dying away. And the Old One lay cold and silent in Roger's hand.

"I will," said Roger. "Right away. I was just going to."

"What did you say?" said Ann, coming into the room in her nightgown.

"Nothing," said Roger, from force of habit. Then he went on quickly. "Yes, I did, too. I was talking to *him*." And he told Ann all about it, and Eliza came in in the middle of it, and asked questions, and he had to start over, and tell it again, from the beginning. Ann believed it right away, the way she always did, but Eliza was disposed to scoff.

"The boy's raving," she said. "Too much reading has turned his feeble brain."

Roger shook his head. "Honest," he said.

"Scout's honor?" said Eliza.

"By my halidom," said Roger.

And of course after that Eliza believed, and was all too ready to run the whole thing, and wanted the magic to start happening right away.

"It can't," said Roger. "Not till tomorrow night."

"Why not?"

"Hast thou sunk so low that thou hast forgotten the good old rule that magic goeth by threes?"

"Well, I think it's silly of it," said Eliza.

"I hate arithmetic," said Ann.

"I think it makes it more interesting," said Roger. "And it gives us time to plan. The first thing is to get the castle back the way it was."

"Why?" said Eliza.

"I think we ought to go by the book. Just to be on the safe side."

"*They* didn't," Ann pointed out. "Once the magic began and you got to be their size, they did just as they pleased. *I* mean to do just as I please from the start!"

Roger began to see what the Old One meant about women.

"After all," Ann went on, "you had your chance. I think we ought to take turns from now on. I get this turn, 'cause I'm your sister. And I don't think we ought to plan at all. I think we ought to build just whatever comes into our heads, and then leave it up to *them*. I think it'll be more exciting that way."

This was such a long and spunky speech for Ann

to make that the others were too surprised to argue.

"I guess it's only fair," said Roger. "Don't say I didn't warn you. Have it your own way."

"Good," said Ann.

"I get dibs on next time," said Eliza.

After breakfast they tried to interest Jack in the magic, but he would have none of it. He said he had too much to do to listen to a lot of nutty talk, and went off to his darkroom to develop the pictures he'd taken to replace the ones Ann had spoiled when she walked into the darkroom yesterday.

Ann and Eliza and Roger didn't mind. They were too busy roaming the house, collecting material for the magic city. An old toy chest in Eliza's room yielded a store of battered playthings, and Ann added toy autos and parts of electric train to the city with reckless abandon. Roger and Eliza invaded the kitchen, and borrowed so many cooky cutters and jelly molds that the cook cried out and said she'd have to speak to the madam.

But Aunt Katharine, except for the times when she was defending her art treasures from the children's eager clutches, was so delighted at how well they were getting along that she made little objection, and, as Ann put it, the hours moved on oiled wheels until pretty soon it was the fateful night. The city by this time was terrible and wonderful to behold. I shall not attempt to tell you what it was like. It defied description.

One thing the children were careful to do, and that was to leave a wide cleared avenue from the hall door to Roger's bed. "Otherwise we might never find each other once it starts," said Ann, "and it'd be like those awful books where the characters get separated and you can't keep track of anybody."

And then she had another idea, and added one final touch. Her final touch was a statue, or at least that's what Ann said it was, to stand in the park in front of the castle. The statue was composed of a can of pea soup, balanced on an iron trivet. It was labeled, "St. George Peabody."

And then it was bedtime. Nobody was sure how far into the house the magic would reach, and Eliza's room was way over in another wing, but that didn't discourage Eliza.

"Meet me by midnight when the lone wolf howls," she whispered to Ann. And as soon as the heavy feet of grown-up interference were safely out of the way, a howl like a rather small and cautious wolf's was heard, and a lone figure came tiptoeing into Ann's room and got into her bed.

"How now, you secret, black and midnight hag?" said the figure.

"Shush," said Ann. "It won't happen if we talk."

But the night when you want to go to sleep most is always the night when you can't, as you may have noticed yourself on nights before Christmas. And not only that, but Ann had decided they should wear their bathrobes and slippers to bed, for Roger had told them how silly he felt, arriving at Torquilstone in just his pajamas and bare feet, and the extra clothes and crowded conditions made things hot and difficult. And not only that, but it was a single bed. And not only that, but Eliza proved to be a tosser and a turner and a talker.

"What do you hope happens?" she whispered. "I hope there's a battle and a siege and we get to rescue somebody from durance vile. Maybe we can fix it so Ivanhoe marries Rebecca, too."

"Shush," said Ann.

"I wouldn't mind having a deadly combat with that Brian, either," Eliza went on, thoughtfully. "Move over. Your elbow's in my back."

Ann sighed, and squashed herself against the wall.

But at long last sleep came and knitted up Eliza's raveled sleeve of care, and after that Ann was still awake for a while, and then all of a sudden she wasn't.

When she woke up she knew it had begun. It was still dark in her room, and her bed hadn't turned into a plateau and was still just a bed, but somehow she knew it was time. She shook Eliza. "Wake up," she said.

"Man the battlements," muttered Eliza, hitting out. "The Normans are attacking."

"You're dreaming," said Ann. "Wake up. This is real."

Eliza opened her eyes and staggered to the door after Ann. And then she wasn't sleepy anymore.

Where the hall should have been there wasn't any hall, just great airy space, and far above them a round shining globe that might have been the hall light back in unmagic times.

And from up ahead, where the door of Roger's room had been, came a blaze of light and a deafening roar. Ann and Eliza ran over drab stubbly earth (the hall carpet had been brown) in the direction of the light and the noise. Then they stopped.

"My," said Ann. "It *is* streamlined, isn't it?"

The magic city had grown to life-size, and the beastlike roar was the sound of its traffic, as all the motorized vehicles from Eliza's toy-chest whizzed about its avenues. And all its buildings were modern with glass and chromium, and glaring with electric lamps and neon signs, and that was the blaze of light. It was like the middle of New York City, only more so. Except that riding the trucks and sports cars and parts of old electric trains were knights in armor and ladies in tall headdresses. Few of them were expert drivers, and all of them were exceeding the speed limit.

Ann eyed the city dubiously. "I didn't think it'd be like this, exactly," she said.

Eliza had no qualms. "Come on!" she cried. "Into the jaws of death rode the six hundred!" And she pulled Ann forward into the heart of the traffic.

A varlet in a Yellow Cab skidded toward them on two wheels and they had to jump for the curbstone.

"Let's find Roger," said Ann.

They looked ahead, and far in the distance they saw a small figure clambering down a fall of rock. They ran toward it. A bus came along, going their way, and Eliza hailed it and pushed Ann up the step before her.

"What about money?" said Ann.

"Who knows?" said Eliza. "Maybe magic will provide."

But it didn't. When they thrust their hands in their bathrobe pockets, nothing was in them but the usual linings and handkerchiefs and cooky crumbs.

"Fares, please," said a guard, appearing beside them firmly.

Ann and Eliza got off the bus.

But they'd already ridden halfway across the city, and the running figure of Roger was much nearer now. A second later he ran up to them. They stood in a doorway, shouting to be heard over the city's noise.

"Isn't this keen?" said Eliza.

"No, it's not. It's horrible," said Roger. He turned on Ann. "What did I tell you? You've just practically ruined the whole age of knighthood, that's all!"

"I know," said Ann. "I didn't realize."

"I don't know what you mean," said Eliza. "I think we've done a noble deed. We've brought the poor things out of the dark ages and given them all the comforts of modern civilization!"

A knight rode by on a motorcycle. He had his fair lady with him, in the sidecar. Roger averted his eyes. "It's sacrilege," he said.

A crash was heard in the distance, as several cars collided. Police cars arrived on the scene, sounding their sirens.

"The only thing is," admitted Eliza, "they don't seem to be very *good* at it yet. Maybe we improved them too *quickly*."

Traffic was now hopelessly snarled, and all the knights and ladies were blowing their horns. A factory whistle screamed, and more knights and ladies emerged for lunch hour, reading comic books and movie magazines. One of the knights jostled against Roger.

"I crave thy pardon, gentle sir," said Roger.

"Get outa the way, stoopid," said the knight, shoving past. From somewhere nearby a band started playing, "Sh-Boom, Sh-Boom."

"This is awful," said Roger. "We might just as well not have come. It's not like magic at all. It's just like ordinary times back home."

"Let's go somewhere where it's quieter," said Ann.

Even Eliza agreed, and the three children turned a corner into a shabby alleyway of small, hutlike houses looking like nothing so much as cardboard boxes hastily painted to resemble stonework.

"I never saw this part," said Ann. "Who built it?"

"I did," said Roger. "It may not be pretty but at least it's more old-time. At least it's more in keeping."

No one was in sight but a veiled lady, stepping toward them. "Good morning, children," she said. "How do you feel?"

"Hello," said Eliza. "I feel all right."

"Have you been vaccinated for contagious diseases?" said the lady. "Have a cough drop." And she produced one from a pocket first-aid kit.

"No, thank you," said Ann. "Are you the district nurse? I didn't know we had one."

The lady threw back her veil, and smiled at Ann and Eliza and Roger with her kind beautiful sad dark eyes.

"Why, you're Rebecca!" cried Ann. "What are you doing here?"

"Visiting the sick," said Rebecca, "and doing good."

"Oh, for Heaven's sake," said Eliza. "The story *said* you went like that in the end. *I* think it's a shame. If you'd only waited, Ivanhoe would have seen the light some day. You could have married him, and visited the sick in your spare time!"

Rebecca shook her lovely head. "It was not to be."

"Then he *did* marry Rowena?" said Eliza.

"Not yet. They are to be married when the siege of Torquilstone is over."

"The siege? Is it still going on?" Roger joined in. "Who's winning?"

"It goes on all the time," said Rebecca, sadly, "and no one ever wins." Then she looked at him more closely. "But I know you! You're Roger! Have you come to save us? The way you did before?"

"Did I?" said Roger, pleased.

"Of course you did. With your Elfish magic."

"I wasn't sure," said Roger. "We elves forget things."

"You saved us," went on Rebecca, "and then you disappeared in a cloud of glory, and then a terrible thing happened. A mighty sorceress cast a spell over the whole country."

"Oh, dear," said Ann. "Did she?"

"Yes, she did," said Rebecca. "And you can see for yourselves what followed. All that noise, and newfangled inventions, and everybody rushing and nobody getting anywhere! Nobody speaking the old ancient yeomanly talk any more, either. You can walk a whole city block without hearing a single 'By my halidom!' And you can imagine what happened to the siege."

"It went to pot," guessed Eliza.

"That's exactly where it went," said Rebecca. "Oh, they still fire a few arrows on weekdays between two and four, but nobody takes it seriously anymore. They let the servants take care of it, mostly." Her voice trembled with emotion. "And Wilfred of Ivanhoe's sword grows rusty and they say he just lies in bed all day and reads science fiction!"

"Why, how perfectly disgusting!" said Eliza.

"I thought you liked it modern, this way," said Ann.

"I don't any more," said Eliza. "I think it's perfectly disgusting."

"It is," said Rebecca. "But now Roger has come back, everything will be changed!"

"What?" said Roger. "Oh, of course. Sure it will. We'll have to do something."

"What'll we do?" said Ann.

"Start a revolution," said Eliza. "Down with progress. Bring back the horse."

"Sort of an Underground Movement," said Roger. "We could have secret meetings."

"With passwords," said Ann.

"I'll be the beautiful female spy," said Eliza.

"Splendid!" Rebecca clapped her hands. "And then when we're all organized, surely Ivanhoe will see the error of his ways!"

"He'd better," said Eliza, "or else!"

They were all so excited by now that they weren't looking around them much, as they walked along. Now Ann did look ahead, and said, "Oh!" in a surprised way, and the others looked, too.

Coming toward them was a knight in armor riding a gallant steed.

"Well!" said Eliza. "There's at least *somebody* around here who hasn't changed!"

"Doesn't he look beautiful?" said Ann.

"Not so dusty," said Roger.

"Just like old times!" breathed Rebecca, with glowing eyes and clasped hands.

But as the knight drew nearer, they saw that his armor was rusty, and his steed, though still gallant, was spavined and rheumy with age. His shield and all his clothing were black, and the visor of his helmet was down, hiding his face. His pace was slow, and he hung his head and seemed a prey to utter melancholy.

"Good morrow, fair lady," he said, his voice coming indistinctly from behind the closed visor. "How farest thou on this dark and dreary day?"

"*He* talks old ancient yeomanly language still," whispered Eliza.

"That I do, lass," said the knight, whose ears seemed to be sharp, in spite of his closed helmet. "A murrain on newfangled inventions, say I! What was good enough for me is good enough for me! By the rood!" he added.

"It doeth my heart good to hear thee speak so," cried Rebecca, falling easily into the old speech, herself.

"Doth it now?" said the knight. "And how goeth it with thy gentle heart this morning?"

"Better than for many a moon," said Rebecca, "now that Roger hath returned."

"Indeed?" said the knight, looking at Roger, and Eliza did not think he sounded pleased.

"That's right," said Roger. "We're organizing everybody who wants to go back to the good old days. You can be our first recruit. What's your name?" Then he didn't think that sounded old-timeish enough. "How call they you, fair sir? And open thy visor, that we may see thy face and know thee friend."

"Nay," said the knight. "I have sworn a vow. My shield be black in mourning for the death of chivalry, and my visor remaineth forever shut that I may not see the light of this modern world till the old days returneth. Men call me the Unknown Knight."

"What a beautiful sentiment," said Rebecca.

"Thinkst thou so?" said the knight. "Then may I be thy champion and fight for thee, and mayhap win thy heart?"

"Nay," said Rebecca, regretfully. " 'Tis too late. Another claimeth it."

"What?" said the knight angrily. "Beateth it still for Wilfred of Ivanhoe, that mewling, puling milksop?"

"Oh sir!" cried Rebecca. "Say not so, for thou woundest my very soul!"

"Milksop I say and milksop he be!" cried the knight, getting excited. "And a mollycoddle and a lie-abed-late and a novel-reader and a space-happy dreamer and a rascally knave of a Saxon churl!"

At this Roger grew hot under the collar and would have spoken up, but Eliza spoke first. "Why, sirrah!" she said. "How thou talkest! Be thee not Saxon thyself?"

"To be sure, lass, to be sure," said the knight, quickly. He leaped from his horse and knelt before Rebecca. "Forgive me, gentle lady," he said. "My righteous anger was too much for me."

Rebecca was touched. "And no wonder," she said. "Thou art too noble, that is thy trouble. I forgive thee readily." And she put out her hand.

The knight seized it and covered it with kisses, pushing his visor part way up to do so. "Blessings on thy kind heart," he cried, "and thy soft dusky cheek, and thy dark eyes a man might drown in, and thy beauty fit to drive a fellow mad!"

"Why, sir!" said Rebecca, drawing back in alarm.

But Eliza, who had been watching the knight closely, stepped up to him suddenly as he knelt, and pulled his visor the rest of the way open. And the knight leaped up and his eyes flashed fire and his mustaches bristled, and even though his Templar's shield was camouflaged with black paint, the three children knew him right away for none other than Brian de Bois-Guilbert, and Roger wished he had brought a sword.

"Oh Rebecca," cried Bois-Guilbert, "vouchsafe me but one smile from thy sweet eyes. Be kind to me as thou wert to the Unknown Knight!"

"Fie, false Templar!" cried Rebecca. "For shame! Thoughtst thou to woo me in disguise and win aught but my scorn?"

"Thou'rt mine now," said the Templar, catching her by the arm, "and none shall come between us!"

"Oh, won't they?" said Roger, squaring up to him and putting up his fists. "Let her go!" And he aimed a blow at Bois-Guilbert's midsection.

"Let her go!" echoed Eliza, running up daringly to trip the false knight from behind.

"Avaunt, moppets!" said Bois-Guilbert, sweeping them from his path with a brutal arm. He smiled cruelly down at Roger as he sprawled on the sidewalk. "Thou and I hast met before, methinks. Had I time, I would settle thy hash now for good and all. Take care that we meet not again." And he leaped to the saddle and swung Rebecca up behind him.

"Wait!" cried Roger, scrambling to his feet and clutching vainly at the bridle.

"You'll be sorry!" said Eliza.

"Oh, yes?" said Bois-Guilbert. "Thou and who

else shalt make me? Thinkst thou any knight in this degenerate age dare follow me to the Dolorous Tower? Because that's whither we goeth!"

"Nay, Templar, not that!" cried Rebecca, in the first words of fear the children had heard pass her lips. And her olive cheek paled.

"Aye," said the Templar, his face set in grim lines. "Brian de Bois-Guilbert dareth even that for thee! Giddy-up." And the spavined steed remembered its glorious past and made a surprisingly gallant dash down the alleyway.

Ann and Eliza and Roger dashed after it, and round the corner into the busy avenue. Far in the distance they saw the horse and its riders disappearing in a cloud of dust. And villain though Bois-Guilbert was, Roger couldn't help admiring the masterful way he was steering his steed through the crowd of badly driven motor cars.

"One thing you have to admit," he said. "He may be a vile dastard but he's still yeomanly!"

"Never mind about that now!" said Eliza. "Come on."

"Where?" said Ann.

"Where do you suppose?" said Eliza. She pointed.

Across the city, the turrets of Torquilstone glittered against the sky. With one accord, the three children turned and ran toward them.

4

The Dolorous Tower

As they ran through the streets of the degraded city, not a single knightly scene met their gaze. Those of the populace who weren't out joyriding were sitting inside looking at wrestling-matches on television. It was sickening.

And when they reached the castle, the state of the siege looked even more sorry than Rebecca had told them. Not a single attacker or defender was in sight. The drawbridge was down and the portcullis was up. The three children ran over the one and under the other and into the courtyard. A discouraging sight awaited them.

Two guards sat playing gin rummy and smoking cigarettes. Their helmets were off and their armor was loosened. They looked thoroughly out of training and unfit for combat.

"Go away," said one of them, without looking up. "All deliveries use the back door."

"We're not a delivery, we're important messengers," said Ann.

"It's a matter of life and death," said Eliza.

The guard yawned. "Mister Ivanhoe is not at home. Come back on Tuesday."

Roger was disgusted at the lax and corrupt behavior of the guards. He banged his fist on the table. "Poltroons, take us to thy master at once!"

"Who are you?" said the guard, insolently.

"I'm Roger," said Roger.

The guard tittered. "A likely story!" he said. "Everyone knows there never was any such person. Nobody believes that old myth nowadays. Nowadays Roger's just a word you use at the end of conversations."

"Roger. Like that. It means oke," said the second guard.

"Oak? Oh, you mean oke," said Roger.

Eliza, who had been fuming at this delay, now burst out. "He is *too* Roger," she said, "and this" —pointing at Ann—"is a mighty sorceress. You'd better let us in or you'll be sorry. I'm a pretty well-known witch, myself!"

The second guard turned to his friend. "Maybe it's true, Perce. They've got on pajamas, the way they say Roger did when he done the deed and won the battle! They talk the old ancient yeomanly language, too!"

"I couldn't take the responsibility," said Percy, for that was the first guard's fitting name. "Not for some old impostors. It's your deal." And he returned to his game.

The second guard winked at Roger. "Run along in, kids," he said. "One flight up and the first door on your right. Don't say we sent you."

And the three children pushed past the guards and ran through the great hall of the castle, shuddering at its new modern glass and chromium furniture, and up the stairs.

The first door to the right was open, and they looked in on a disillusioning spectacle. For a minute even Eliza was speechless.

Wilfred of Ivanhoe, in dressing gown and slippers, lay on a couch deep in study. He still wore a bandage round his middle, and he also wore a pair of horn-rimmed spectacles. His face looked pale and thin and scholarly. He was reading a book with a red cover, and every so often he stopped and made a note. Roger recognized the book at once. It was called *The Angry Planet*, and he had brought it with him from home, and Ann had used it when she built a public library for the Magic City.

Across the room from Ivanhoe sat Rowena. She had grown much plumper, and was lolling in an armchair, eating chocolate-covered cherries.

"My dear," Ivanhoe was saying, "did you know that Mars is only one-third as big as the earth and so the force of gravity is only one-third as strong?"

"Pass the stuffed dates," said Rowena.

Ivanhoe didn't hear her. He was making a note. Rowena sighed. Then she put on a coaxing expression. "Ivanhoe, when will the siege be over? When will we be married?"

"One moment, my dear," said Ivanhoe. He finished working out his arithmetic problem. "Amazing! That would mean that the Martians must be eighteen feet tall. Otherwise they'd bounce."

"Not necessarily," said Roger from the doorway. "They might be made of something heavier than we are. They might be made of lead. They might be wide instead of high."

"Don't talk so fast," said Ivanhoe, his pencil traveling madly over the paper. "I can't get it all down."

"Who are you?" said Rowena. "How dare you enter this chamber unannounced?"

"I'm Roger," said Roger.

"You don't say?" Ivanhoe looked up with a smile of welcome. "Come in, my dear fellow! Forgive my not getting up. My old wound still troubles me. Sit down. I'm delighted to see you. The old stories always *said* you'd come again some day. To finish the siege, but we don't have to talk about that now, do we?"

"Yes, we do," said Rowena. "I'd *like* to talk about it. You said you'd marry me when the siege was over, but how can the siege be over if you never fight?"

"Please, my dear," said Ivanhoe. "Not now. Roger must have lots more interesting things to tell us. Coming from Elfland, he must know all kinds of things. Tell me"—and he turned to Roger again— "how high exactly *is* the moon?"

"The moon," said Roger, promptly, "is two hundred and thirty-nine thousand miles from the earth. Approximately."

"Fascinating," said Ivanhoe. "Is it inhabited?"

"I don't know," said Roger. "Nobody knows."

"Then you can't be Roger," said Ivanhoe. "Roger knows everything."

"Not quite," said Roger, modestly. "I'm only in six-one-A. Now about that siege."

"I'm afraid my fighting days are over," said Ivanhoe. "My old wound, you know."

"Wilfred, that's just your imagination," said Rowena. "That old wound must have healed by now. Goodness knows I make you enough bandages, don't I?"

"Not like the kind Rebecca used to make," said Ivanhoe.

Rowena looked hurt. "Wilfred!" she said. "I thought we agreed never to mention that name!"

But the mention of Rebecca had roused Eliza from her spellbound silence at the door. "Oh, for Heaven's sake!" she interrupted. She marched straight into the middle of the room and stood looking down scornfully. "Wilfred of Ivanhoe, you get right up this minute!" she said. "While you're just lying there, Brian de What's-his-name has kidnapped Rebecca!"

"What?" Ivanhoe leaped up. "Why didn't you say so before?"

"I was just going to," said Roger, sheepishly. "I kind of got sidetracked."

Ivanhoe strode across the room, his eyes flashing

fire behind their spectacles. "Perfidious wretch! He shall die for this!"

"Now, Wilfred," said Rowena, following him fussily, "it isn't as if it were the first time. In my opinion people who go round getting themselves kidnapped don't deserve a bit of sympathy! You don't see anyone kidnapping *me*, do you?"

"No," muttered Ivanhoe, "I certainly don't." He was rummaging in a corner. "Where is my new armor? What have you done with my helmet? What is this sticky stuff all over my best sword? Have you been using it to toast marshmallows again?"

"Wilfred," said Rowena, "you get right back on that couch. You're not well."

"A minute ago you wanted me to get up and fight."

"A minute ago," said Rowena, "was different."

"Tush to thy puling," said Ivanhoe, falling into the old yeomanly talk now there was occasion for it. "Hold this cuirass."

"I won't," said Rowena.

"All right, *thou* holdst it, then," said Ivanhoe to Ann, who was nearest. And Ann reached up and held it for him to put on, feeling very romantic and like a lady in a storybook.

The armor was a bit large for him, now he had grown thinner, but he looked quite knightly in it, particularly after he took off his spectacles, which he did because they wouldn't fit under the helmet. "By my halidom!" he cried, when the armor was all on. "I feel like a new man! My old wound scarce troubleth me at all!"

Eliza nudged Roger, and Roger formally introduced Ivanhoe to Ann the mighty sorceress and Eliza the well-known witch. Ivanhoe assured them he was honored, and made a low bow and kissed their hands, while Ann and Eliza giggled, and blushed, and tried to make grand sweeping curtsies, and looked, in Roger's opinion, very silly.

"And now," said Ivanhoe, "where hath the vile villain taken her?"

"To the Dolorous Tower, he said," said Eliza, "wherever that is."

Ivanhoe turned pale, as Rebecca had before him. "It lieth in the Outer Wastes, beyond the edge of the world," he said.

"You mean in Outer Space?" Roger's eyes glowed.

Ivanhoe nodded. "Thou mightst say that it doth. In a way."

"Golly!" said Eliza. This adventure was getting better and better, after all.

Ann didn't think it was. She thought it was getting worse and worse. But before she could say so, there was an interruption.

"That settles it!" said Rowena to Ivanhoe. "You're not going gallivanting off into any Outer Space after any old Rebecca! Why, you might never come back!"

"That's true," said Ivanhoe, brightening and sounding as though he rather liked the idea. "I might never! Besides," he went on, "this giveth me a good chance to try out my Flying Saucer. I've always wanted to."

"Flying Saucer?" cried Ann, in utter alarm. "You don't have one of *those*, do you? Don't look at *me*!" she said quickly to Roger. "I didn't put *that* in!"

"I know," said Roger. "*I* did."

"Then you're just as bad as I am," said Ann.

"Come along," said Ivanhoe.

"Stop!" said Rowena, barring their way, but they pushed past her and went down the stairs and through the courtyard and out of the castle.

Ann, who had never so much as been up in an airplane in all her eight years and three months, was a prey to conflicting emotions. She didn't want to go up in a Flying Saucer, but she wanted even less to say so, because that would be putting herself in a class with Rowena, which was not a place where she ever wanted to be.

And now Ivanhoe was leading them behind the castle, and there the Flying Saucer waited, lashed down and straining at its moorings like a live thing.

Eliza recognized it at once. "Why, that's part of our breakfast set," she said. "It's Wedgewood."

"Edgeworld," Ivanhoe corrected her. "A pretty thought, is it not? I thought of it. It saileth over the edge of the world. Gettest thou the point?"

"Yes," said Ann, with sinking heart. "I do."

An attendant with a white beard helped them up the ladder into the Saucer. This time Roger recognized him. It was the Old One. He did not speak, but winked at Roger and Eliza, and gave Ann an encouraging pat on the head. This comforted Ann a little, but not much.

They took their places on the rim of the saucer, Ann between Roger and Ivanhoe. "What makes it go?" Roger wanted to know.

Ivanhoe shook his head. "I know not. I never dared ride it before." This did not add to Ann's confidence.

The next minute the mechanism, whatever it was, started, and she was thrown heavily against the armored Ivanhoe, who hurt. And the *next* minute they rose, spinning, straight up in the air.

At first the sensation was horrible, like a thousand Empire State Building elevator rides mixed up with a thousand merry-go-rounds, but by the time the machine gained its top speed it was revolving so fast that the children hardly realized it was turn-

ing at all, any more than you feel the earth turning
under your feet, as the schoolbooks would have you
believe it does.

After a bit Ann took courage to look down over

the edge. She saw the castle and the city fast disappearing below, and before them not the ghost of shores, before them only shoreless skies.

"This is super," said Roger, hanging his head over the edge next to her, and shouting against the wind.

"Is it?" said Ann.

"Look!" said Eliza, pointing.

They looked. Far above and ahead of them, but coming nearer every second, hung a round shining globe.

"The moon!" cried Eliza, in tones of wild excitement, and "The moon!" cried Roger, in tones of awe, and "The moon!" breathed Ivanhoe in such a tone as Columbus might have used on a certain famous occasion.

"The moon?" said Ann, doubtfully. It didn't look quite right to her. It reminded her of something else.

"We can make it if we just keepeth on," Ivanhoe was saying.

"What about Rebecca?" Ann reminded him.

"Ah yes. I was almost forgetting," said Ivanhoe, with something almost like regret.

"Too bad," said Eliza.

"Maybe some other day," said Roger.

They all peered down over the edge again. The city had vanished, except for a faint glow in the far distance. Otherwise there was nothing to be seen but vast, airy, empty moonlit nothingness. "We had best land at once," said Ivanhoe. "We be over the edge of the world right now."

"How do we make it go down?" Roger wanted to know.

"I know not," Ivanhoe admitted. "What thinkst thou if we all make ourselves as heavy as we can, and then bear down hard?"

This didn't seem very scientific to Roger, but strange to say, it did the trick. The Edgeworld plunged straight downward in the neat habit of all Flying Saucers, with no sissy business of gliding and banking, like your mere airplanes, and at last, after what felt like a thousand *more* Empire State elevator rides (only going down this time, which is far worse), it came to rest as lightly as a large feather on something that felt pleasantly like solid earth.

"Where are we?" said Eliza, clambering down the portable ladder and looking round at the scenery (only there wasn't any).

"The Outer Wastes," said Ivanhoe.

"No, it isn't," said Ann, jumping down and feeling the familiar stubble underfoot. "It's the hall. . ." But she was interrupted.

"Hist!" said Ivanhoe, a little distance away. "Hark!"

They harked. From somewhere not far off a voice was speaking, and it was the voice of Brian de Bois-Guilbert.

And then, only a little way across the stubbly plain, they saw a tower built all of yellow metal, palely shining in the moonlight. And inside the tower Rebecca languished in durance vile, while Bois-Guilbert stood outside looking in at her, and uttered a cruel laugh.

" 'Tis the Dolorous Tower!" whispered Ivanhoe. And he and Roger and Eliza and Ann moved stealthily nearer.

Bois-Guilbert stood with his back to them, and he didn't turn around as they crept close. "Relent, Rebecca," he was saying. "Proffer me but one kind word, else I must leave thee to perish in this lonely prison on this blasted heath."

"Nay," said Rebecca.

"Rebecca," said Bois-Guilbert again, "think what thou art saying! Do not force me to do this dread deed, for it grieveth me greatly. Only smile on my suit, and thou art free. And if thou lovest me not yet, mayhap thou canst learn."

"Never," said Rebecca.

"Rebecca, for the third and last time," said the Templar, getting exasperated, "stop being so stubborn! Recollect that thou art my prisoner, alone and with none to aid thee!"

"Not so," cried Ivanhoe, stepping forth into a shaft of moonlight, so that he shone all silvered on the darkling plain. "Turn, Templar, and meet thy end!"

"What?" said Bois-Guilbert, turning angrily. "Who asked thee to interrupt? How camest thou hither, anyway? Never mind," he added quickly, as Ivanhoe started describing the Flying Saucer. "Don't tell me. I don't want to hear about it. Back to thy books, stargazer, ere I make thee see stars of a different color!"

"Bully!" cried Roger, stepping forth next to Ivanhoe.

"Fiend!" cried Eliza, stepping forth next to Roger.

"Shame on you!" cried Ann, stepping forth on the end of the line.

When he saw the three children, the Templar's dark visage whitened. "What, thou again?" he said. "And thou and thou? Witch brats, do I have to find ye in my path every time I'm just getting started? Surely 'tis an evil omen and ye were born to be my bane! Nonetheless, I fight!" And he fell upon Ivanhoe with naked sword.

And there raged such a conflict, on that dark

heath, as has seldom been seen outside the pages of romantic fiction. Steel rang on steel and harsh cries sounded. Bois-Guilbert thwacked Ivanhoe and Ivanhoe thwacked him right back again. Roger and Eliza jumped up and down in excitement. Rebecca clung to the bars of the prison, her eyes shining. Ann watched with clasped hands.

The slow minutes passed, filled with clashes and grunts and heavy breathing. For a long time none could say who would be victor on that bloody battleground. And though one was good and one evil, none could help but admire the fighting form of both.

Then, at last, training told its tale.

Too long had the limbs of Ivanhoe lain stretched in studious ease upon his couch; too long had he stayed absent from the courts of tourney. Besides, he didn't have his glasses on and he couldn't see. Too long had his keen eyes been strained with poring over stirring tales of interplanetary travel and scientific experiment.

A mighty blow of the Templar's sword brought him crashing to his knees. He dropped his sword. Then he couldn't see to find it. As he crawled on his hands and knees, vainly looking for it, the Templar took careful aim.

"Take care!" cried Rebecca, from within the tower.

"Do something!" said Ann, her fingers digging into Roger's arm.

"I can't. Can I? It wouldn't be right. Would it?" said Roger. "Two against one?"

"At a time like this," said Eliza, "who cares? All is fair in love and war!" And she ran to Bois-Guilbert and tried to find a gap in his armor, to bite him.

But it was too late. The Templar's sword came crashing down on Ivanhoe's helmet in a mighty blow, and the hapless hero sank unconscious beneath it.

"Now for the death thrust," said Bois-Guilbert, pulling out his dagger.

"Help him, Roger," called Rebecca from the tower. "Use thy Elfish magic!"

"I would if I could," said Roger, "but I can't. I don't have any. Honest I don't. That's all a mistake. I'm not an elf. I'm a boy."

"Farewell to hope, then," said Rebecca. "Spare his life, Templar, and I am thine!"

"No, don't do that! Wait!" cried Eliza.

"Hocus pocus," muttered Roger. "Might as well try anything once. Abracadabra. Allez-oop." He stopped to see if anything magic would happen, but of course nothing did.

Ann was sniffling. Roger was pale. Eliza was gritting her teeth. Then suddenly her face cleared.

"What are we so worried about?" she said. "It isn't as if they were real. They're nothing but a lot of lead soldiers!"

"Stop!" Roger opened his mouth to cry, but it was too late.

"What didst thou say?" said Bois-Guilbert, dropping his sword.

"What didst thou say?" said Ivanhoe, coming to and sitting up and looking around.

"Lead soldiers, lead soldiers, lead soldiers!" said Eliza.

"The Words of Power!" cried Rebecca, from the Dolorous Tower. "The Elfish Magic!" And right away the disappearing began.

Ivanhoe and Rebecca and Bois-Guilbert grew dim and then transparent, and then they simply weren't there at all, and the gray mist came swirling down and blotted out everything, and the next Roger and Ann and Eliza knew, they were sitting on the floor of the hall outside Ann's door, looking at some toy knights and a saucer and a yellow tin wastebasket upside down with a toy lady standing on top of it, and a round shining globe that was no longer a moon but just a hall light.

"The Outer Wastes," said Roger, pointing at the wastebasket. "The Dolorous Tower."

"What happened?" said Eliza.

"You said the Words of Power," said Roger. "Didn't I tell you about them?" And he told her about them now.

The children's mother chose this moment to appear in the hall.

"Up playing at this hour, the idea," she said. "It's one o'clock in the morning. How did that saucer get on the floor?"

"It flew there," said Ann, stupidly. She was still dazed by the suddenness with which the adventure had ended.

"This," said their mother, "is no time for funny jokes. Roger and Eliza, go back to your own rooms. Ann, go to bed. You've all been dreaming. And I only hope you haven't started walking in your sleep, too, because that would be the Last Straw!"

After that there was really nothing to do but trail back to their separate rooms. Roger knocked some of the Magic City over as he trailed through his, but he didn't care. It had been a mistake. If there were any more adventures and if he had anything to say about them, they were going to be yeomanly, like the first one. Magic and modernness just didn't mix.

Eliza, on the way to *her* room, was thinking about the battle and how thrilling it had been. She wondered if Ivanhoe had lived to tell the tale, and if Rebecca had ever got out of the Dolorous Tower, and what had happened next.

Ann, in her bed in *her* room, was wondering the same thing, and wondering if she would ever know the answer.

"Magic things goeth by threes," she said to herself. "Does that mean the next adventure'll be the last one?"

She was still wondering when she fell asleep.

———

The Greenwood Tree

Roger woke up the next morning to a chinking and a clinking and a coming and going of feet, all adding up to what he recognized all too well as the sound of Putting Away.

He opened his eyes and looked across the room. The Magic City was gone, except for the castle in one corner with a part of the park and the statue of

St. George Peabody, and the dollhouse in the next corner, and some fake trees along the wall in between, and Prince John's court in the fireplace.

And in the middle of the room stood his mother, gazing round at her handiwork as though she found it good.

Roger sat up in bed. His mother met his accusing look. "I know," she said, defensively, "but it just Had To Be. Think of the poor maid who's supposed to clean in here."

At this moment Ann came rushing in from the hall. "They're gone!" she cried.

"What are?" said their mother.

"Who?" said Roger.

"Ivanhoe and Rebecca and that Brian." She turned on their mother. "What did you do with them?"

Their mother gestured vaguely toward the castle. "Whatever I found I put over there somewhere."

"Oh! Now we'll never know how they would have got back if you hadn't!" Ann wailed.

"Honestly!" said their mother. "You'd almost think the things were *alive*!"

Ann and Roger exchanged a look.

On the way to breakfast they met Eliza. She was full of excited plans. "What'll we do next?" she said. "It's my turn this time, 'cause I said dibs on it. What'll we make happen tonight?"

"Nothing," said Roger. "We can't." And he reminded her about magic going by threes.

"It would!" said Eliza, bitterly. "You'd almost think it *tried* to make things harder! How'll we exist in the meantime?"

"The meantime of what?" said Jack, coming into the dining room behind them.

"You wouldn't believe it if we told you," said Roger. And they proceeded to.

Luckily the custom at Aunt Katharine's was the sensible one of having the children eat by themselves, except on special occasions; so they were able to tell Jack all through breakfast with no fear of grown-up scoffing, and spill as much maple syrup as they wanted to, in their enthusiasm, without the tyranny of table manners to interrupt.

When they'd finished they could see he was impressed.

"*Now* do you believe in magic?" said Ann.

"There might be something to it," Jack admitted. "Maybe not magic, exactly. Maybe kind of extrasensory perception, more. Maybe next time I'd better come along. Look at it scientifically."

"Huh uh," said Roger. "No more science."

"Not that old science fiction stuff, *real* science," said Jack. "Examine the facts. I'll bring my camera."

"That'll be nice," said Ann.

They all went up to Roger's room. "Just where did it happen?" said Jack, looking around and sniffing the air, as an inquiring photographer and scientific detective should.

"It's no use. It's too late. Mother picked up," Ann told him bitterly.

"That reminds me," said Roger. He went over and investigated the castle. Their mother had piled the soldiers every which way in the keep, and it took a long time to get them sorted.

Eliza was boss, because it was her adventure next. Under her direction, they put Robin Hood and the Black Knight and Maid Marian and some Merry Men out among the fake trees, and lined up De Bracy and his followers in besieging formation outside the castle again. They stood various courtiers and attendants about the lower chambers (Rowena was still sulking in her upper one), but they couldn't find Ivanhoe or Rebecca or Brian de Bois-Guilbert anywhere.

"Let's get the Old One," said Ann.

"Who's he?" said Jack.

They told him.

But when Eliza took the Old One from the castle, and asked him what had happened to Ivanhoe and the others, he didn't answer, and at first he was so cold in their hands that they were afraid the magic was over for good. Jack was beginning to look skeptical when all of a sudden the Old One *did* warm up a little, as though to show them it wasn't over, but that was all he would do.

"Interesting," said Jack, feeling the warm Old One. "Peculiar phenomenon. Probably some quality in the metal. Retains heat."

"Why wouldn't he answer?" said Ann.

"Maybe we're not meant to know," said Roger. "Maybe we're meant to not do anything about it, and just wait till the third night."

"That's going to be hard," said Ann.

"Hard," said Eliza, "is not the word. I for one shall go raving tearing mad."

But it turned out that she didn't. And the three days passed quicker than you would have believed. Once you're friends with people, it's surprising how much you can find to do with them, even without magic to Light the Way.

Roger went on learning about photography from Jack, and met some of Jack's friends and hacked around with them, and played a lot of baseball and in general decided Jack wasn't really half so bad as he had painted him.

Ann didn't have such an easy time. With Roger so busy, she was left to Eliza's tender mercies, and the difference between eight years old and eleven-and-a-half loomed large. But Eliza was surprisingly nice, and offered to play hopscotch with her, and jacks, and one day she gave a tea party for Ann, and asked all her friends to meet her.

Ann was grateful, though she didn't enjoy the conversation much, which was mostly about which boys on the block were the best-looking. Nor did she prove proficient in dancing the Lindy, when the big girls tried to teach her how. She would rather have stayed in her room and investigated her new dollhouse, but she suppressed this thought. Eliza, she felt somehow, would disdain it.

And at last the third night came.

There had been some worry about sleeping arrangements, but their mothers were so pleased at what good friends they were getting to be that they raised no objections when Eliza wanted a cot put up in Ann's room, and Jack asked to sleep on Roger's couch.

That night four bathrobed figures assembled before the castle. It had been a big day of baseball, and Jack got down on the floor now and started moving De Bracy and his followers around in different formations, demonstrating how Roger could have won the game if he'd played differently.

"Don't!" said Ann. "Once you start moving them around you never can tell *what* might happen!"

"What could happen?" said Jack.

"Almost anything," said Eliza. "You don't know what that magic's like when it's roused!"

"Ah, don't pay any attention to them," said Roger suddenly and basely, full of his new manly importance as Jack's friend. "They're just a couple of crazy girls."

After that, Ann did not take much part in the conversation.

Eliza's reaction to being called a crazy girl was different. In the process of her reaction a chair leg came off and the floor was scratched, but no one was seriously hurt.

"One thing I've been wondering," said Roger, when peace had been restored. "Why doesn't the Old One ever talk to us when we run into him? I mean, when we meet him in the magic part. All he ever does is kind of smile and wink."

"Yes," said Eliza. "You'd think he could at least give us advice and steer our faltering steps."

"Maybe he can't," said Jack. "When you see him in the magic part—I mean the old-time part," he corrected himself, for he still wasn't ready to admit the magic was real, "why, then he's in *his own time.* He can't get out of it into yours, any more than you can get into his."

"But we do," said Eliza.

"Not ackcherly," said Jack. "You're still yourselves, all the time you're back there. You're not really part of that time at all. You're sort of just visiting."

All this about two kinds of time was too deep for Ann. And when she said so, and Jack tried to explain, Roger betrayed her again.

"She won't get it," he said. "She's too young."

Ann felt depressed. Not only was she a girl, but she was too young. There didn't seem to be much future for anybody who was both these things. She gave Roger a wounded look, and turned away from him to the others. "Isn't it bedtime?" she said.

"For once in my life," said Eliza, "I wish it were."

"We could set the clock ahead," suggested Roger. He felt a little guilty and smiled at the back of Ann's neck, trying to make her turn around, but she wouldn't.

Jack shook his head. "That's no good. It wouldn't be scientific. Might spoil the whole thing."

So then Ann said she was going to bed anyway, and Eliza went with her. And then Roger remembered to warn Jack about the Words of Power; so he wouldn't use them by accident, and cut off the adventure in full flower, the way Eliza had. After that he tried to think whether there were anything more he should tell Jack, and there didn't seem to be. He forced a yawn. "Ho hum," he said. "Might as well hit the sack, too."

"What for?" said Jack. "It's early."

"I just guess I will," said Roger. And he got into bed.

If the truth must be told, he was feeling sorry for the things he'd said about Ann, and the way she had looked after he'd said them. The sooner the magic began the sooner everything would be right again.

Jack went on talking to him from across the room, but Roger shut his eyes and began taking long breaths, pretending he was asleep. Pretty soon, as so often happens when you do this, he was.

Jack strapped his camera on, in readiness for whatever striking scene might occur, and lay down on the couch, but he still felt wide awake. After a bit he got up and tiptoed across the room and stood looking down at Roger. Roger's eyes were shut.

And reassured that Roger wasn't awake, to see him being so childish, Jack tiptoed over to the fake trees near the castle, and knelt down and started playing with Robin Hood and his band, for all the world as though he were a boy of eleven, and not a man of nearly thirteen.

He had the Merry Men hunt a deer. Then he had them hold an archery contest. Robin Hood won easily, by shooting the petals off a daisy, one by one.

After that, Jack lay back on the carpet. He'd just stretch out here a minute, he told himself; then he'd get into bed. Strange as it seemed and early as it was, he felt suddenly very, very sleepy.

When Roger woke up and saw the familiar plateau stretching around him and knew that the magic was happening, he scrambled to his feet and hurried down the rocky path to the plain below. Far away toward the horizon he made out two dim figures hurrying toward him. Roger ran and the figures ran, and they met on the greensward.

"I'm sorry," were the first words of Roger.

"What for?" said Ann.

"You know," said Roger.

"What are you talking about?" said Eliza.

"Nothing," said Ann, but she felt better. "Where's Jack?"

"He slept that way," said Roger, pointing at a far plateau that had been Jack's couch. The three of them hurried across the plain. But as they neared the plateau, they couldn't see any sign of human habitation. And when they came right up to it, they saw that the plateau was smooth and unruffled, as though it hadn't been slept on all night.

"If that isn't just *like* that magic!" Eliza cried indignantly. "It got to him ahead of us. He's probably somewhere in the middle of it right now, being scientific and ruining *my* adventure! Come on!"

"Where?" said Ann. "We don't know where he is, or Ivanhoe, or anybody!"

"Start with the castle," said Roger. "That's always the beginning of everything. Our Social Studies book says in medieval times the castle was the hub of all activity."

The three of them ran toward the familiar towers of Torquilstone. As they hurried through the park, they could see figures moving up ahead.

"The siege must be still going on," said Roger, pointing.

"Oh, is that what they're doing?" said Ann. "That isn't what it looks like."

And now, as they drew nearer, the others saw that Ann was right. What was going on didn't look like a siege at all. A ball came hurtling through the air, but it didn't seem to be a cannonball, exactly. Some sort of stick flashed in the sun, but it didn't seem to be a pikestaff, or a quarterstaff, either.

And then they were very close, and loud voices rang on the bright air.

"He striketh thrice!" cried the first voice, in loud, official-sounding tones. "Out upon him!"

Other voices interrupted angrily. "Nay!" they cried. "A pox on thee! 'Twas a ball! Slay the Umpire!" And all the figures surged together in a quarreling knot.

Roger and Ann and Eliza came to a halt near some varlets who were looking on. "What's happening?" Roger asked one of them.

"It be ye sport of Base Ball," said the varlet. "The Norman team claimeth a ball but the Umpire saith them nay. It be ye olde Rhubarb."

"Good grief," said Roger. "Has the siege come to this? This is worse than last time."

Ann did not say "I told you so" to her brother. She merely gave him a meaningful look.

"Jack ought to be here," said Eliza. "He'd be in his glory. Where do you suppose he is?"

"Never mind about that now," said Roger. "The point is, who's winning?"

"It be a tie," said the varlet. "Naught to naught in ye sixth."

And now the quarrel (or rhubarb) seemed to be over, and the Saxons and Normans straggled back to their positions. A dignified-looking, white-haired gentleman who seemed to be the Umpire tossed the ball back into play, and the children saw that it was the Old One. He raised his eyebrows at Roger, but did not speak.

Meanwhile a tall Norman had stepped up to home plate, swinging his bat. At sight of him a murmur ran through the crowd. Some cheered and cried, "Up the Normans!" while others booed.

"Who is it?" hissed Roger to the varlet.

" 'Tis the greatest Norman of them all," said the varlet. " 'Tis Babe De Bracy. 'Tis ye Sultan of Swatte."

And then, as all eyes were fixed on the mighty Norman, a shameful thing happened. The Lady Rowena appeared on the battlements of the castle, no longer slothful and chocolate-fed, but slim and lovely, her blonde hair streaming on the wind. And as Roger and Eliza and Ann watched, horrified, she waved a lily-white hand at De Bracy. The mighty batsman bowed low in her direction, and she blew him a kiss.

"Why, the traitorous thing!" said Ann. "Imagine!"

"Isn't that just like her?" said Eliza.

The booing from the Saxon fans, which had grown louder when the Lady Rowena appeared, died down, and again Babe De Bracy approached home plate, his bat swinging.

But again there was an interruption. The portcullis of the castle moved upward, the drawbridge creakingly descended, and two figures advanced across it, on horseback. One was bearded and elderly, and the three children recognized him right away. It was Cedric the Saxon, Ivanhoe's father. Wamba the jester rode by his side.

De Bracy left the baseball diamond and strode over to the two horsemen. "What meaneth this?" he said. "Doth the castle surrender?"

Cedric the Saxon drew himself up proudly. "Never," he cried, "while breath remaineth in me to defend it! I but crave leave to depart to seek my vanished son."

"Thy son is dead, methinks," said De Bracy, "else why hath he not returned?"

"Dead fiddlesticks!" cried Rowena, appearing suddenly on the drawbridge beside them and interrupting. "Run off with that Rebecca, more likely!"

"Temper, temper!" said Wamba.

"Peace, fool," said Rowena.

"For shame," said Cedric the Saxon, glaring at Rowena. "Smiling on the enemy and making thy great eyes at him from the very battlements of our Saxon stronghold, I saw thee!"

"I must needs smile at someone," said Rowena, "and none other was forthcoming. Besides, all the ladies smile at the Sultan of Swatte." And she batted her eyes at De Bracy.

"Faugh!" said Cedric the Saxon. "I shall find my son, if he be living, and he shall return to save our merrie land from these degenerate games. Sultan of Swatte, indeed! My son shall swatte *thee*!" And he turned his haughty glare upon De Bracy.

"Take care, gaffer," said the Norman. "Who cometh begging favors must needs speak more discreetly. Nonetheless, none can say Maurice De Bracy was ever an ungenerous foe. Depart in peace and seek thy son. But proceed with caution, for thou art old and thy fool but a fool." He strode back to the baseball diamond. "Play ball!" he cried, and the game began again.

Ann and Roger and Eliza ran after Cedric and Wamba. "Wait!" Roger called. "Take us with you; we want to find him, too!"

The two riders reined in their horses. " 'Tis Roger!" cried Wamba. "And the witch and the sorceress with him! Now surely we are in luck, for they have come to set us on the right path."

"Lead me to my son, elf-child," said Cedric the Saxon, "and I shall bless thy name forever."

"I can't," said Roger. "I don't know where he is."

"We know where he *was*," put in Ann, "but he's not there any more."

"Then surely my son is dead," cried Cedric, "if the magic of Elfland itself cannot find him!"

"Not necessarily," said Roger.

"You'd be surprised what all we don't know," said Eliza.

"We know he's not *that* way, though," said Ann, pointing ahead through the park toward the greensward and the distant plateaus. "We've *been* there."

So Cedric the Saxon and Wamba turned their horses toward the grove of trees on their left, and Roger climbed up with Wamba, and Cedric lifted Eliza and Ann up to ride with him in a kind of double pillion, and they set off to look for Wilfred of Ivanhoe.

As they went along, the trees grew thicker and taller till they found themselves in a deep forest. The earth was carpeted with acorns and beech-mast, and the sunlight, sifting through the foliage above, turned the air the color of new young leaves; so that it was a green wood indeed. Once a deer galloped across their path, looking so free and beautiful and lordly that Ann and Eliza and Roger caught their breaths in sheer wonder.

It was a second after that that they heard a twanging sound, and something they thought was a bird flew by, over their shoulders. Only then they knew that it hadn't been a bird, because there was another twanging sound, and an arrow suddenly thrilled in the heart of an oak tree just ahead.

They pulled up short, their hearts beating fast. All at once the forest seemed alive with laughing men in green jerkins and hose. And in the midst of them, and grinning at Eliza and Roger and Ann, stood a familiar figure.

"Isn't this swell?" it said. "I guess there ackcherly *is* magic, after all."

When Jack awoke after going to sleep on the carpet, he found himself lying on cool grass at the edge of a wood. For a minute he couldn't think where he was; then he remembered. He jumped to his feet and walked into the wood, swinging a stick he fashioned from a fallen oak branch, and wondering what was going to happen next.

What happened next was a twanging noise in his ear, and something came flying through the air, straight at him. There was no time to duck, but he'd always been a good man with a fastball; so he quickly took his stance, and struck at the flying thing with his oak staff.

And he wasn't the batting champion of several Baltimore, Maryland, vacant lots for nothing. His stick hit the flying thing squarely, but instead of sailing over the fence and out, as it would have if it had been a baseball, it just stuck there on the end of the stick, and when he looked at it he saw that it was an arrow that had gone halfway through the stout oak.

The next thing he knew, a handsome man in green had appeared from behind a tree and was applauding him.

"Well played, boy!" said the man.

"Thanks," said Jack.

"But what is thy business in Sherwood Forest?" the strange man went on. "And art thou rich or poor, that I may know whether to rob thee or call thee friend?"

"Sherwood Forest?" said Jack. "Gee. Of course. And you're Robin Hood."

The man in green bowed. "Naturally."

A thrill went through Jack, and he reached for his everready camera. This would be the best picture yet. Not only that, but it would prove the magic had been real, afterwards.

"Hold still a second," he said. "Smile, please. There." And he clicked the shutter.

"What be yon?" said Robin Hood. "Some new-fangled wizardry or other?"

"Sort of," said Jack. "I'll send you a copy if it comes out. Gosh. Robin Hood. Could I shake your hand, sir?" And he held his own hand out. "My name's Jack."

"Well met, Jack!" said Robin Hood, gripping it manfully. "With thy quick eye and thy ready hand

and wizardry besides, thou shouldst go far in the outlaw trade. Wouldst care to join my merry band?"

"Oh boy!" said Jack. "Wouldst I ever!"

Robin Hood blew a blast on his hunting horn, and outlaws appeared from behind every tree; Maid Marian in a green gown, and Will Scarlet in scarlet, and Allan-a-Dale with his lute, and a huge fellow who could only be Little John. And after that, Jack didn't care whether the magic were real or not. Whatever it was, it was super.

Then, just as Robin was taking Jack around and introducing him to his comrades, another bowman in green came running into the clearing and stood there, getting his breath back.

"What news, Will Stutely?" said Robin Hood.

"Travelers approaching, sir," said Will Stutely. "On horseback, and richly caparisoned, to judge by the jingling!"

"Oho!" said Robin Hood. "More rich booty to plunder and divide among the deserving poor! To your posts, gentlemen!"

There was a sort of flicker, and Jack rubbed his eyes. Except for Robin Hood and himself, not a soul was to be seen. Robin clapped him on the shoulder. "Thy first taste of outlawry, boy!" he said. "Keep by me." And he whisked Jack behind an elm, where they lay crouched together as the unsuspecting horsemen moved into the clearing, jingling as they came.

Only the jingling wasn't caused by rich caparisons, but by Wamba's jester's bells, and when Robin Hood saw who the horsemen were he laughed mightily (but silently) in Jack's ear.

"Marry, 'tis old friends," he breathed. "Nonetheless, we shall give them a scare, for old times' sake." And fitting a shaft to his bow, he sent it whirring past the travelers, and then sent its fellow deep into the heart of an oak tree directly in their path.

"Help!" cried Wamba, falling off his horse and then trying to hide under it.

"Indians!" cried Ann, who wasn't thinking.

"No, it isn't; it's . . ." began Roger. But at that moment Robin Hood jumped laughing out from behind his tree, and the other outlaws jumped laughing out from behind theirs, and Jack came grinning up to Ann and Eliza and Roger.

When Robin Hood heard of Ivanhoe's disappearance he swore a mighty oath, and when he heard that Roger himself had come again, to join in the search for the missing hero, he came up to Roger and bowed low before him.

"Sir," he said, "this is a great honor."

"Oh, that's all right," said Roger. "It's mutual."

"Thou art too kind," said Robin Hood. "We must have a feast to celebrate the occasion. Men, roast the deer!" And the hearts of the four children thrilled at these truly yeomanly words.

"Is there time, though?" said Roger. "Shouldn't we get searching?"

"Searchers require sustenance," said Robin Hood. "Tonight we feast. Tomorrow we join in the hunt."

"I crave thy pardon," said a tall figure in black armor who had appeared out of the shadows. "Didst say Wilfred of Ivanhoe was lost while on some deed of derring-do? Hath the moon-mad dreamer then recovered from his stargazing?"

"Don't blame him. That wasn't his fault," said Roger. He pointed at Ann. "This mighty sorceress here did that."

"Then death to her," said the Black Knight, putting his hand on his sword.

"Oh dear," said Ann.

"Nay!" said Roger, quickly. "She hath reformed."

"She'd better!" muttered the Black Knight. But he took his hand off his sword. "And Wilfred is the old knightly Ivanhoe once more?"

"Well." Roger hesitated.

"Of course he's a little bit out of practice," said Ann.

"But the last time we saw him, he was rescuing a maiden," said Eliza.

"My, my, just like old times," beamed the Black Knight. "I feel like a new man. Richard is himself again!"

"Sire," said Roger. "I've been wondering. Why don't you come back to your throne and drive Prince John and the Normans out and make everything good again?"

"Marry, mayhap I will!" said Richard. "If the old age of chivalry returneth, who am I to be behindhand? Must find dear old Wilfred first, however. After that, who knoweth?"

So that night all was feasting, and if Ann and Roger and Eliza found the taste of roast venison disappointing (maybe because of the deer they had seen all alive and beautiful in the forest), at least they were too well brought up to say so. And dessert, which was wild strawberry junket and frumenty, was dandy.

After the feast, toasts were drunk and songs were sung, and they all lay back in the shade of the spreading greenwood tree and Jack wished this magic, if that's what it was, would go on forever.

And then the strange thing happened. A bird

fluttered into the clearing and all around the company, almost brushing their faces with its wings, before it flounced to a perch on the limb of a nearby oak. And somehow all of them knew that this was no ordinary bird.

" 'Tis a falcon!" said Little John.

"With its jesses broken and trailing, the poor strayed thing!" said Maid Marian.

"And if I mistake not, with some paper or other tied unto them," said Robin Hood, striding from his place to look up at the bird. "Could it be 'tis a message for someone here present?"

And now everyone was clustering around the falcon in the tree, and making what everyone hoped were reassuring noises.

"There, there," said Maid Marian.

"Nice falcon," said Ann.

"Soo, boss," said Much the Miller, who was of a rustic background.

The falcon merely fixed them with its glittering eye.

"Wait," said Robin Hood. And he climbed the tree as one who knew no fear, and the falcon seemed to respect this, and allowed itself to be carried to earth with no struggles, or biting and tearing. Robin Hood untied the paper and glanced at it. Then he gave a cry, and read it aloud:

"To Whom It May Concern:
"We are all three of us prisoners
in the Giants' Lair. Help.
(Signed) Wilfred I.
Rebecca Y.
Brian de B. G."

Immediately the air was filled with a babble of excited talk.

"My son!" cried Cedric the Saxon.

"Giants! Ugh! Sooner them than me!" cried all the outlaws.

"Brian de Bois-Guilbert?" said the Black Knight with a snort. "Is Wilfred hobnobbing with *that* dastard?"

"It's not his fault," Roger told him. "They were fighting together the last time I saw them. They probably got taken prisoner together. He probably won't like being rescued by us any more than we'll like rescuing him. It's probably just a case of any port in a storm."

"Where's this Giants' Lair?" said Jack.

Robin Hood looked grave. "It lieth beyond the forest, at the world's end," he said. "Rumor hath it that the giants who dwell therein are ogres of the most deadly variety, though of course I have never seen them, myself. Few have, and lived to tell the tale. Indeed the legend runneth that no man may enter that grimly habitation of his own free will."

"How do we save them then?" asked Roger.

"The one creature for whom 'tis said the door standeth ever open," said Robin Hood, "is a little girl."

Eliza pushed forward eagerly. After all, this was supposed to be her adventure.

Robin Hood looked her over. "Thou mightst do," he said, "but little still would be better."

All eyes turned to Ann. Ann felt small. "You mean me?"

"To a mighty sorceress," said Robin Hood, "all things should be possible."

"Yes," said Ann dubiously, "I suppose they should."

"We of course," went on Robin, "would accompany you as far as possible, stand by to be of what aid we can, et cetera."

"What about me? Can't I go along?" asked Roger. Ann threw him a grateful look.

"Under certain circumstances," admitted Robin, " 'tis said that a small boy also may enter those hideous halls."

"Me too?" asked Jack.

Robin Hood looked at him, and there seemed to be a twinkle in his eye. "Thou art grown near to man's estate, boy," he said. "But while the legend runneth that the door standeth open only for a little girl, there is another legend that only a certain youth may conquer the dread monsters within. I should say that if the lady meaneth to undertake this journey, she would do very well to have thee along!"

"Good," said Jack. He grinned at Ann, and winked.

"Count me in," said Roger. "Me, too," said Eliza.

Everybody seemed to be waiting for Ann to say something. She looked round at them all, and swallowed. She thought of how much she liked Ivanhoe and Rebecca, and how, even though Brian de Bois-Guilbert might be wicked as wicked, he was still a knight and deserved a knightly death, not one at horrid giant hands (or teeth). And she hoped she sounded brave, because she didn't feel brave at all.

"All right," she said. "I'll try."

A cheer burst from the lips of Robin Hood and his men. Eliza threw her arms round Ann. Jack thumped her on the back.

Ann looked at Roger. Roger looked at Ann. "Pretty good," he said, "for a girl."

And that made Ann feel best of all.

The Giants' Lair

Once the die was cast, Ann wanted to start for the Giants' Lair right away and get it over with, and so did Roger and Jack and Eliza. But Robin Hood shook his head.

"Ye must rest and store up your strength," he

told them. "Who knoweth what ordeals ye may un-
dergo before ye see old Sherwood again?" And Ann
and Roger and Jack and Eliza had to agree that who
knew, indeed?

But getting to sleep that night was not easy for
any of them, particularly Ann, even though their
couches were of fragrant bracken and their pillows
scented with pine needles, and even though Maid
Marian came and told them soothing stories of the
sunnier side of outlaw life.

And when Ann finally did drop off, she had the
most bloodcurdling dreams all night.

But the forest birds woke them cheerfully in the
morning, and tomorrow was, as usual, another day,
and all was swash and buckle as they made ready
for the journey, and then all too soon they *were*
ready, and the procession started off through the
trees, in the opposite direction from Torquilstone
Castle.

At first the going was easy, and foxgloves glowed
like purple and white candles, and birds warbled
their native woodnotes wild, and Allan-a-Dale sang
tirra lirra, and Ann might almost have believed they
were bound on a party of pleasure, instead of a deed
of derring-do.

But as the day wore on things got different. No
more flowers bloomed under the trees, which were

mostly dead or blasted by lightning, anyway. And around their splintered trunks hung stringy, thorny briers that slapped the travelers scratchingly in the face and seemed to be trying to hold them back. The sun went behind a cloud. A thin cold wind blew down their necks. A carrion crow flew over.

"We're getting near," said Robin Hood.

And Ann and Eliza and Roger and Jack could see that the forest ended just ahead, not thinning out and trailing away gradually, like a respectable forest, but stopping suddenly, as though all life had been cut off at one fell swoop.

"The Giants' Lair!" said Robin, pointing.

Ann and Eliza and Roger and Jack knew what they expected to see—a grim, half-ruined castle like one of the drawings of Mr. Charles Addams in *The New Yorker*, with bats flying around and toads on the terrace and a wolf at the door, and maybe a horrible head glaring from a window.

They stopped at the edge of the forest.

"Hideous, isn't it?" said Robin Hood. "Like nothing ever built by human hands!"

Ann and Eliza and Roger and Jack looked. It wasn't like a Charles Addams drawing at all. Except that it was about a hundred times normal size, what they saw was a perfectly ordinary house, such as you might see in any perfectly ordinary suburb today, with white paint and green blinds and a neat lawn and flowerbeds.

Maid Marian averted her eyes. "How dreadful!" she shuddered. "Robin, can we leave these innocent children to go in there alone?"

"There's nothing wrong," said Jack. "It's just a house only it's too big."

"It's just like any old house back home," said Eliza, disappointed. "I think it's boring."

"There's no accounting for tastes," said Maid Marian.

Ann didn't say anything. There was something familiar about the house, but she couldn't think what it was.

"And now," said Robin Hood, "this is where you must leave us. We shall be waiting here if there be any little thing we can do."

"Good luck," said Marian, kissing Ann.

"Tell old Wilfred chin up from me," said the Black Knight.

"Save my son," said Cedric the Saxon.

"We'll try," said Roger.

He and Eliza and Ann and Jack got down from their horses.

"But stay," said Robin Hood. "I was forgetting. Thou bearest no arms."

"Do we have to?" said Ann. "I'd rather not."

"I wouldn't," said Eliza, swaggering.

Robin Hood looked at them. Again there seemed to be a twinkle in his eye. "Methinks," he said, "that Jack at least should bear some weapon."

The Black Knight stepped forward, and in this moment he looked every inch King Richard the Lionhearted. He drew his sword from its sheath. "This blade," he said, "hath fought right valiantly against Saracens abroad and traitors at home. Take it, and may it do yet one more bright deed for Merrie England."

"Thanks a lot," said Jack.

And he and Roger and Eliza and Ann started walking across the lawn.

But as they drew nearer the house it kept looking bigger and bigger, and the four children felt smaller and smaller in the middle of the vast grassy expanse. There were no fierce cries from within and nothing pounced at them out of the front door. But they felt better when they gained the shelter of a hedge at the side of the house. And beyond the hedge they saw a cellar window.

The window was open what probably seemed only a crack to it, but to small Ann and Roger and Jack and Eliza it was a great yawning cavern. They slithered through the hedge, ran forward stealthily, crouched on the vast sill and looked into the room below.

What they expected to see was a grisly dungeon, with chains, and somebody grinding somebody else's bones to make his bread. That would have been unpleasant, but only to be expected. But that wasn't what they saw at all.

What they saw was a perfectly ordinary-looking rumpus room. If it hadn't been so big it might have looked rather jolly. If the people in it hadn't been so big they might have looked rather jolly, too.

They were a man (if you could call him that) and a woman (or at least a female) and a little girl (if you could describe as little a being that was at least four times as tall as Jack). Their cheeks were of a pink-and-white, china-like perfection, and their eyes were blue and staring, with long curling lashes, and their lips parted, showing pearly teeth.

And no matter what they said or did, they never stopped smiling. After a while, Ann wished they wouldn't.

There was something else peculiar about the room, too. There didn't seem to be enough furniture to go round. And Ann noticed that the train of the female giant's red velvet gown seemed to have been cut away, leaving a jagged edge. And the man giant's tail-coat didn't have any tails. And the little girl giant had blonde corkscrew curls on one side of her face, but on the other side she didn't have any. And suddenly Ann knew the secret of the Giant's Lair. She turned to Eliza to tell her.

"Shush," said Eliza. "Look." And she pointed.

The giant family was squatting down now, and gazing at something on the floor, but Ann couldn't see what it was. Then she heard a piteous voice.

"Oh, please do not play with me any more!" it cried. "I am so tired!" It was the voice of Rebecca.

And far down on the floor, the four children made out the forms of Ivanhoe and Brian de Bois-Guilbert, standing one on each side of Rebecca as though to protect her.

The voice of the female giant now made itself heard.

"Why, the very idea! What impudence. Don't you pay a bit of attention to what the horrid little thing says. You play with them. Play just as hard as you can. Play house with the girl and soldiers with the boys."

"Yes, Mama!" said the child giant. And she picked Rebecca up and started undressing her, and then got tired of that halfway through and put her down in a draft, and took hold of Ivanhoe and Bois-Guilbert instead, and started marching them up and

down the floor in a childish and elementary manner.

Ann and Roger and Eliza looked at each other
with indignation.

"It's an insult to the whole order of knighthood!" sputtered Roger.

"*I* think it's an outrage!" said Eliza.

"What have those giants got there? Dolls?" said Jack.

"No, that's Ivanhoe and Rebecca and Bois-Guilbert," Ann told him. "It's dolls that have got *them*!"

For of course that was the secret of the Giants' Lair. It was the neglected dollhouse Aunt Katharine had given Ann, that she had never played with, except to plunder its rooms when she was furbishing the Magic City.

"I knew there was something wrong with that dollhouse the minute I saw it," Eliza was saying now to Ann.

"You're right," said Ann. "They're not nice dolls."

The little girl doll (or giant) now decided to play war and make Ivanhoe and Bois-Guilbert have a deadly combat. She did this in crude fashion by holding one of them in each hand and then knocking them together, hard.

"Sorry, old man," said Bois-Guilbert. "Was that my boot in thy left eye?"

" 'Twas not thy fault, old fellow," said Ivanhoe. "Oops! Did I crack thy crown? Blame not me. Blame this monstrous child."

"I do," said Bois-Guilbert. "I blame her more than I can say. And more of the same from her I will not suffer!" And he drew his sword and attacked the giant child.

Of course to her it was as the prick of a mere pin, but she immediately dropped both knights on the floor (stunning them badly) and began to cry, in the whining tone of all crying dolls.

"Mama," she cried. "It hurt me!"

"Why, the vicious thing," said her mother.

"We won't have any more of *that*!" said the father giant. "They are not fit pets for you to play with! They should be destroyed!"

At this the child giant began to cry louder, but her mother soothed her. "Wait," she said. "I have an idea. Come with me, and Mama will put some iodine on your finger, and then we will come back and Papa will get his pliers and remove their stings. Then you may play with them just as much as you want to."

And the child giant suffered herself to be led away, her father pausing only long enough to put Ivanhoe and Rebecca and Bois-Guilbert on a table, for safekeeping.

As soon as they'd gone, Eliza said, "Pssst."

Rebecca looked around the room.

"Up here," said Ann.

Rebecca's eyes found the window, high up near the ceiling, and her face lighted. " 'Tis Roger!" she cried. "And the witch and the sorceress with him!"

"Then haply we may hope again," said Ivanhoe.

"Oh Roger," said Bois-Guilbert, humbly. "Thou and I hast crossed swords more than once in days of yore, but fetch us out of this prison and I shall atone for my many sins!"

"Well, for Heaven's sake!" said Eliza, in surprise. "How you've changed, haven't you?"

"We'll save you all if we can," said Roger. "Anyway, we'll try."

"Wait there," said Jack.

"We needs must," said Ivanhoe, peering down from the table. "Other choice offereth there none."

Roger and Ann and Jack and Eliza scrambled out from their perch on the windowsill (for the drop from there was even higher than the drop from the table) and ran around the house looking for a way to the cellar. At last they found some steps leading down, with a door at the bottom.

"For a little girl," said Roger, "the door standeth ever open."

Even as he spoke and even as they looked, the door swung wide of its own accord. But getting to it was another matter.

"Take a giant step," said Eliza, bitterly, looking down at the series of perilous drops before them. But they managed it at last by hanging from the edge of each step with their hands, and then letting go. They arrived at the bottom, whole but somewhat jolted.

And once in the cellar, they faced the problem of how to get Rebecca and Ivanhoe and Bois-Guilbert down from the table.

"Use thy Elfish magic," suggested Ivanhoe.

"You don't ever seem to understand about that," said Roger. "There isn't any. At least there is, but we can't use it. We're sort of *in* it!"

But it was vain to attempt to explain. "Come, come," said Ivanhoe. "Thou art merely being modest."

"Think how thou hast saved us in the past," said Rebecca.

"Our fate is in thy hands," added Bois-Guilbert, piously. "Heaven hath sent thee to us in our hour of need."

After that the children had to think of something, and it was Ann who saw the end of a skein of yarn hanging down from the table, where the female giant had been knitting, and it was Jack who had the strength to pull a whole mass of the great floppy stuff down to the floor, and it was Roger and Jack who made the rope ladder, and it was Eliza who looked on and told them how to do it. Ann kept watch at the door.

"Sister Ann, what do you hear?" said Roger.

"Awful screams," said Ann. "They're putting on the iodine."

"Good," said Eliza.

At last the ladder was ready, and Ivanhoe and Bois-Guilbert, pulling as hard as they could on the other end of the yarn, managed to heave it up to the table.

"Ladies goeth first," said Ivanhoe to Rebecca.

"Nay," said Bois-Guilbert. "One of us strong men should precede her, to aid in her descent and break her fall shouldst she tumble."

"What a goodly thought, old man!" said Ivanhoe. "Go thou, and I shall come third."

"Not at all, my dear fellow," said Bois-Guilbert. "After thee!"

"My, you two certainly are pals all of a sudden," said Roger.

"We have sworn brotherhood," said Ivanhoe. "Brian is a new man. He hath reformed."

"Rebecca hath reformed me," said Bois-Guilbert. "It helped to pass the time. Besides, what is chivalry for, if two knights do not unite against a common enemy? Old Wilfred and I have been through thick and thin together in this dungeon."

"There is a great deal of good in old Brian," said Ivanhoe. "We are . . . What was the word Roger hath used?"

"We are pals," said Bois-Guilbert, gripping Ivanhoe by the hand.

"Good," said Eliza. "Now let's hurry."

But which of the two knights would finally have gone down the yarn ladder first will never be known. For now heavy feet were heard on the stairs, and the three smiling giants appeared in the doorway. They stood looking around the room.

"Someone has been leaving the cellar door open," said the father giant, crossing to shut it.

"Someone has been snarling up my knitting," said the mother giant, seizing the yarn ladder and pulling it apart beyond repair.

"Someone has been trying to steal my playthings," cried the little-girl giant, "and there they are now!" And she pointed at Roger and Jack and Ann and Eliza.

"Well, well," said her father. "More pets for you to play with. Aren't you the lucky girl?" And he leaned over to pick up Ann.

Ann's heart quailed, though she tried not to let it. And Eliza stepped forward courageously.

"Don't you touch her!" she said. "You'll be sorry! She may not look it, but she's a mighty sorceress.

It just so happens I'm a pretty powerful witch, my-self. Beware!"

"And I," said Roger, drawing himself up to his full small height, "am the great Roger. You've prob-ably heard of me."

"No," said the giant, "I haven't. And what's more, I don't believe you." And he leaned over them again with his menacing smile.

"Help!" cried Eliza, in sudden alarm. "Jack! Use your sword!"

Jack brandished the blade King Richard had given him.

The giant's face retreated quicker than it had advanced. "What did you say?" he said.

"I told him to use his sword," said Eliza. "He will, too."

"But what was that you called him?" said the giant.

"Jack," said Eliza. "That's his name."

The child giant screamed. The mother giant turned pale.

"I don't believe you," said the father giant again, but his voice trembled. "If that's Jack, where's his beans?"

This time it was Roger who understood. "He's not that Jack," he said. "He's the other one. He's Jack the . . ."

"Don't say it!" cried the giantess, clutching her offspring to her. "Not before the child!" The three giants gazed at Jack in terror.

"What's the matter with them?" said Jack.

"They think you're Jack the Giant Killer," said Ann.

"Okay," said Jack. "What do I do? Kill them?"

Roger looked doubtful. "Do you suppose we have to?"

"Think of the blood," said Ann. "So *much* of it!"

"Only it'd probably be sawdust," said Roger.

"And they'd probably go right on smiling," said Eliza. "I couldn't stand it."

While this discussion was going on, the father giant had been edging toward the table. Now he suddenly caught up Ivanhoe and Rebecca and Bois-Guilbert and held them high in the air.

"I'll teach you to come invading people's homes with your nasty murdering friends," he said. "If he doesn't put away his sword, I'll smash them to smithereens."

Ann and Roger and Eliza gazed up in horror at their captive friends. Jack was so startled that he dropped his sword on the floor.

"Pay no heed," called Rebecca to Jack, from

somewhere up near the ceiling, which was of sky-scraper height. "Take up thy blade!"

"If we die, 'twill be in a good cause," said Ivanhoe.

"I have been a miserable wretch," said Bois-Guilbert, his voice muffled by the giant's hand, but with a sincere ring in it. "But at least I repented before 'twas too late."

"Wait," said Roger to the giant. "Can't we talk this over sensibly? Maybe we could work out some kind of truce."

"What makes you so mean?" said Ann. "What have we ever done to you?"

"Well, really! Well may you ask," said the mother doll (or giant). "It isn't that we mind being played with day and night and wheeled in baby carriages till it's monotonous. Oh no! Nor being undressed and put to bed when we aren't sleepy, and dropped on our heads and left out in the rain, either! That's just part of the normal scheme of things. It's what we were made for. We even enjoy it, in a way. It makes us feel Somebody Cares! But *you*"—her voice trembled and she sounded hurt—"never played with us at all!"

Ann blushed and felt ashamed of herself but Eliza was scornful. "I certainly didn't," she said. "I wouldn't stoop to it."

"Very well," said the mother giant. "Very well. That's your privilege. But when it comes"—and her voice swelled with righteous wrath—"to invading our privacy and spoiling our interior decoration and cutting up the very clothes off our back, why *then* I say it's time to draw the line, and it's no wonder we're striking back! And don't pretend you didn't do it," she went on, pointing at Ann's hand with the birthstone ring with the tiny agate, "because I'd know that hand anywhere! And *that*"—she pointed at Eliza's hand with the bitten fingernails—"is the hand that helps it!"

"Only now they've got little," said the child giant.

"And now," said the father, snatching up Jack's sword from the floor, "they're in our power."

The giant family glowered down at Ann and Eliza.

"What have you done with my red velvet train?" said the mother giant.

"My coattails?" said the father giant.

"My side-curls?" said the little girl giant.

"My fur coat? The best bath mat? The drawing room armchair? The kitchen curtains? The roses from the quilt?" said all three.

Ann blushed guiltily. "I'm sorry," she said.

"We didn't think you'd mind," said Eliza.

"Mind?" said the mother giant. "Mind? Have

we no feelings? Have we no hearts? Are we things of wood and china?"

"Give us back what you stole," said the father giant. "Then maybe we can talk of truces."

"We can't," said Ann, unhappily.

"We don't have them anymore," said Eliza.

"Then bid your friends good-bye forever," said the giant. And again he raised Ivanhoe and Rebecca and Bois-Guilbert in the air, to dash them to pieces on the floor.

"Wait!" cried Ann. "We'll find them for you! We'll bring them back!"

"We'll go on a quest!" said Eliza.

But there was an interruption. "Ah, what does it matter?" said Jack, forgetting for a moment that he had shrunk to toy-soldier size and remembering only his boyish scorn for girls' playthings. "They're just a lot of dolls, anyway!"

"Don't!" cried Roger and Ann and Eliza in one voice, gripped by the same horrid fear. But they were too late.

For these words proved just as powerful as others that shall be nameless, and the mist rolled down, and the giants and Ivanhoe and Rebecca and Bois-Guilbert started growing transparent, and the last thing Roger and Ann and Jack and Eliza saw before everything disappeared completely was the whole wall of the Giant's Lair sort of swinging out and away from them, as though they were in an earthquake.

The next they knew, they were standing in Roger's room looking down at an open dollhouse. Inside the dollhouse were a father doll and a mother doll and a little girl doll and the small figures of Ivanhoe and Rebecca and Bois-Guilbert, lying where the children's mother had put them when she picked up, three days ago.

"Oh!" cried Ann, looking at Jack with a face of utter displeasure. "You might know some *boy* would spoil everything!"

"How was I to know?" said Jack. He turned to Roger. "That's not what you said the Words of Power were."

"It's the same principle," said Roger. "You might have guessed. I did."

"I don't see how," said Jack.

"Maybe he used his head," snapped Eliza. "And this was supposed to be my adventure and you spoiled it before I got to be leader at all, hardly."

There was a silence.

"Robin Hood was keen, though," said Jack.

The others looked at him coldly. "And now he's still waiting at the edge of the wood for us to come back, and maybe we never will!" said Ann.

"Ivanhoe and Rebecca and that Brian'll be killed, of course," said Eliza, joining in in that spirit of making everything as gloomy as possible that can be such a pleasure at such times.

"And the Normans'll win the siege, and the whole thing'll be ruined," said Roger.

"I don't see that it's my fault at all," said Jack. "You can't expect an experiment to come out right if people don't give you the right facts."

"Oh, leave him alone," said Eliza, pityingly. "He's too old to know better."

And they did.

The Quest

"Now then," said Eliza. "What'll we do?"

It was the next day, and hope reigned again in the hearts of the four children.

"Well, the first thing," said Ann, "is to remember all the things we took out of the dollhouse, and find them and put them back."

Eliza shook her head. "That's too easy. Better wait till the magic starts again and go on a quest, like I said."

"But we'll never find all the things when we're small," Ann wailed.

Roger was firm. "Eliza's right. Any other way would be just sissy and cheating."

"But Ann's partly right, too," said Jack. "We can't move all that furniture if we're soldier-size."

"We'll have to compromise," said Roger.

"What's that?" said Ann.

The other three proceeded to show her what it was by taking Prince John's throne from behind the sliding fire screen and putting it back in the dollhouse, where it became the best parlor armchair once more. And all the other furniture that would be too heavy to move, later, they put back now, but the smaller things they left where they were, to be quested for when the magic began.

"I get to plan the quest," said Eliza. "Last time doesn't count as my turn at all. The door stood open for Ann, and Jack nearly was a giant killer, and Roger was the great Roger. I hardly did anything."

And the others all saw that to agree would be the way of much less resistance.

"We ought to make a list," Eliza went on, "of all the things we have to find, and take it along, to prod our sluggish brains."

"I'll get my notebook," said Ann.

"*Can* we take things?" Roger wondered. "We never have."

"We take the clothes we're wearing," said Eliza, "if that signifies."

"And I took my camera," said Jack.

"You did? I never noticed," said Eliza.

"I forgot about it myself," said Jack. "I only took that one picture of Robin Hood, and then I forgot all about developing that."

"Let's go do it now," said Roger. And the two boys departed for the darkroom while Ann and Eliza worked on the list.

"What did we use the father giant's coattails for?" Eliza tried to remember.

"I can't think," said Ann. "I know where the child giant's side-curls went, though." She giggled at the thought of where they had gone. Then she ran to get her notebook, but she couldn't find a pencil (as who ever can?) and the talk turned to other matters.

Pretty soon Roger and Jack came back and reported that the picture of Robin Hood hadn't turned out.

"It must have been overexposed," said Jack, but Roger thought there might be more to it than that.

And so the rest of that day and all the next one passed in fun and games and harmless ploys, and always the fateful third night drew ever nearer. And as to what it might bring, Eliza decreed that they should try not to even think about it. Because planning had never paid in the past, nor meddling, either.

It was on the afternoon of the third day that the telephone call came. Roger and Ann's mother answered it, and after the first few words she turned perfectly white. "Yes," she said. "Yes. Of course." Something about the way she said it made everybody in the room stop talking in mid-word and look at her. Then she hung up.

Aunt Katharine went to her quickly and they left the room together, and could be heard murmuring in low voices in the hall. The four children sat in silence in the living room, where they'd all been playing rummy when the call came, and Ann and Roger remembered other low voices that had gone on and on, that day back at home, and they were worried.

And then Aunt Katharine came back in and told them that it had been the hospital calling, and that the doctors had decided their father had to have an operation right away, today.

"Your mother's going straight out there now," she said. "I'm going with her." And she went to the phone to see about getting a room at the hospital where she and the children's mother could stay tonight till the worry was over.

Roger and Ann went upstairs to find their mother. The three of them didn't talk very much, but each one knew how the other two felt, and Roger and Ann were quiet and helpful about such things as packing their mother's bag for her and remembering what she ought to put in.

Their mother didn't even say good-bye, just kissed them both hard. And then she was gone. And pretty soon Jack and Eliza came upstairs, and the four of them drifted into Roger's room and sat, and nobody said anything much, but you could tell that Jack and Eliza were feeling friendly and sympathetic and wondering what they could do to help, and yet there didn't seem to be anything.

After a while Eliza got red and stared at the floor and said, "Look. Does the magic *have* to happen tonight? Maybe you'd rather it didn't. Maybe it could be indefinitely postponed."

"No," said Roger, unhappily. "Even if it could, it can't," he went on, not very clearly.

"Don't worry about us," said Jack quickly. "We'll understand."

"Sure," said Eliza. "Maybe I could have my adventure next week. Maybe we can fix it with the Old One."

"No, don't do that!" said Roger. "It's *got* to be tonight!"

"Why?" said Eliza.

But Roger looked so desperate that Jack gave his sister a surreptitious kick, and she did not repeat her question. Instead she asked if Roger and Ann would like to take a walk, but Roger said he thought they ought to stay, in case there were a message. And guessing that maybe they wanted to be alone, Eliza and Jack went away.

And when they'd gone, Roger told Ann a thing he'd been keeping to himself all this time. He told her about the wish he'd made that their father would get well in Baltimore, Maryland.

"And the Old One said wishes have to be earned," he told her anxiously. "And you see I *haven't* earned it, and this is my last chance. This is a warning."

Ann's eyes grew solemn. "Let's talk to him," she said. And she went and found the Old One and held him in her hands and stroked him lovingly, and after a while he rather reluctantly warmed up and began to speak.

"Ods fish," he said. "Degenerate times, generation of vipers, posterity is just around the corner and welcome to it! Canst thou not decide a single thing for thyself any more? Have courage and steadfast hearts gone down the drain, pardie?"

"It isn't that," said Ann. "We try. And we mean well, but something always happens."

"Ah yes," said the Old One. "Good intentions. Forsooth we all know what road paveth itself with *them*! On the other hand, if at first thou succeedeth not, try subsequently. And never forget the good old rule that magic goeth by threes."

"Can't you tell us any more, sir?" said Roger. "We *know* that."

The Old One gave him rather a sharp look. "Dost thou?" he said. "Art thou sure?" Then his eyes grew dreamy and his voice seemed to come from farther away. "Meseemeth I remember an ancient rune for just such cases as thine," he murmured. "How didst it run? Ah yes." And he recited slowly:

> "Sword from stone the hero taketh—
> Then the snowbound sleepers waketh!
> Wisdom then the hero learneth!
> Wishes then the hero earneth!"

And after that he wouldn't say another word, and he grew cold and heavy as lead (which he was) in Ann's hand.

"What did all that mean?" said Roger, as Ann put the Old One back in the castle. "Swords in the stone? That's the wrong story."

"And snowbound sleepers," said Ann, "only there aren't any. We didn't put any snow in. Did we?" But she wrote the ancient rune down in her notebook, anyway.

It was a few minutes after that that the phone rang. It was their mother. She said the operation was over and everything was fine so far. Roger sent a silent look of gratitude in the direction of the castle and the Old One. So far, so good.

And then Jack and Eliza came in from their walk, and Roger and Ann showed them the ancient rune, and they couldn't figure it out, either, though they all tried till dinnertime and all through dinner and after dinner, and Jack even consulted his book on secret codes, to no avail.

"Maybe there's more in it than meets the eye," said Eliza. "Maybe it doesn't mean what it says. Maybe it's kind of symbolic. Maybe it's something else we're supposed to quest for. Something that looks like a sword or a stone."

"What looks like a stone besides a stone?" said Ann.

Nobody knew. And then all of a sudden the hours, which usually moved on laggard feet on magic nights, decided to cooperate for once, and it was bedtime.

Roger stayed awake for a while after the others, in case the telephone should ring again, but it didn't. All was still, save for the breathing of Jack on his couch. The gentle rhythm lulled Roger, and soon he knew no more. And soon after that the magic began.

The four cousins met on the usual greensward. Four pairs of eyes shone with eagerness and four hearts beat faster with the excitement of the quest. Where to begin was the question of the hour.

"I remembered one thing," said Ann. "I know where the red velvet train went, and part of the fur coat, too. Cedric the Saxon's got them on."

"And he's way over in Sherwood Forest," said Roger, "and the other things are in the castle, mostly."

"We'll have to separate," said Jack.

"Who'll go where?" said Ann.

"You and Jack take the castle," said Eliza, assuming command. "I'll go with Roger. Then each fair lady will have a champion to save her from worse than death, whatever that is."

"Are you nervous?" said Ann to Roger, privately.

"Yes," he admitted.

"I know," said Ann.

"So much depends on it," said Roger.

"Yes," said Ann.

"What depends on what?" said Eliza, coming up to them.

"Why, the quest depends on us," said Roger. But that wasn't what he was thinking of.

And now all clasped hands in a solemn good-bye. "Good luck," Roger said. "Watch out for Normans." And he and Eliza turned toward Sherwood.

Ann and Jack watched them out of sight; then they set off for Torquilstone.

As they drew near the castle and passed through the park with the statue of St. George Peabody, the rose trees pinkly perfumed the air.

"There's something we can start with," said Ann. "The roses from the quilt." She checked off an item on the list in her notebook, and they both started picking.

"Did you plant this many?" Jack asked after a while.

"I don't see how we could have," said Ann, wearily.

"They must have spread." They went on picking. Then suddenly a hand seized Ann by the shoulder. She turned in its grasp. A guard stood eyeing them sternly. He wore a peculiar uniform Ann had never seen before.

"Picking flowers in public parks is forbidden by the Leader," he said. "Punishable by twenty years' imprisonment. You are under arrest."

"But I put them there in the first place!" cried Ann. "I am the mighty sorceress!"

"Magic," said the guard, even more sternly, "is *specially* forbidden by the Leader. Punishable by burning at the stake, at *least*. Guards, ho!"

But before more guards could appear, Jack grabbed Ann's hand. "Come on," he said, and clutching their armfuls of roses to them, they ran. The guard gave chase, but they dodged among the shrubbery and lost him.

"What do you suppose has happened?" Ann whispered pantingly as they ran. "Who's this Leader?"

"I don't know," Jack whispered back. "Something terrible must have gone wrong."

"After we were so careful, too," said Ann. "You'd think that magic did it on purpose!" And after that she saved her breath for running.

The park was left behind now, and they were on unfamiliar ground. Then, just as Ann reached her last gasp, they saw a sort of great high-ceilinged building ahead, with black iron hangings pushed back at the sides, and they knew where they were.

Jack pulled Ann to a stop. "Lurk!" he whispered. "Maybe we can find out what's up." And they crept toward the curtained chamber, lurked behind the nearest drapery, and peered through its iron folds.

Prince John stood in the middle of the room, surrounded by more oddly-uniformed guards. He wore a peculiar-looking cap on his head, and he was in a fury.

"Answer me!" he was shouting. "Who hath stolen my throne?"

"We know not, oh Leader," said a guard, raising his arm in a peculiar salute.

"Then find out!" snapped Prince John. "What was the use of my seizing the throne in the first place if ye let the first Tom, Dick or Harry who cometh along steal it the moment my back be turned?"

Ann and Jack looked at each other. Now they knew who was Leader in England, and why England was no longer merry.

Then Jack thought of his camera. This was too good a shot to miss. He reached for it, took careful focus, and Ann heard him snap the shutter. Unfortunately Prince John heard him, too.

"A spy!" he cried. "Seize him!"

Rough hands grasped Jack and dragged him from his hiding place. Other hands seized Ann and dragged her after Jack. And at that very moment the guard who had tried to arrest them in the rose garden came puffing up behind them, just to make things worse.

"Hold them!" he cried. "They be both of them mighty sorcerers. The small one hath confessed it."

"Mayhap 'tis they who hath stolen the throne," suggested a guard.

"Their garb is strange, like to that of Roger," whispered another.

"Silence!" cried Prince John. "Hath not thy Leader forbidden that name to be mentioned? There is no Roger." He glared at Ann and Jack and saw the camera. "What be yon devil's instrument?"

"It isn't," said Jack. "It's a camera. I just took your picture. And there is too a Roger. He's my cousin."

"What a camera may be," said Prince John, "I neither know nor care. But making pictures behind this iron curtain"—and he pointed to the draperies—"is punishable by death. So is believing in Roger, let alone being related to him. To the dungeon with them. They shall be burnt at sunrise."

And Ann and Jack were dragged away.

"How did it happen? Where did all these terrible new ideas come from?" Ann said to Jack as they were hustled along. "*We* certainly didn't put them in!"

1 6 1

"Maybe they just sort of leaked in from the out-side world," said Jack. "Goodness knows there's enough of them around!"

The dungeon, when they got to it, proved to be so full already that they could hardly squeeze in.

"No wonder," said Jack, "with practically all the pleasures of life forbidden now!"

"Exactly," said the nearest prisoner. "I could not agree with thee more!"

Ann recognized him right away. It was the Nor-man knight, Maurice De Bracy. "What are *you* doing in jail?" she asked. "I thought Prince John was a friend of yours!"

"No longer," said De Bracy, grimly. "Now he calleth himself Leader, he is no man's friend. He hath become the worst tyrant in history. Some of us fellows finally got up a little petition against him."

"Sure," said Jack. "I know. The Magna Charta."

"Why, yes. How didst thou guess? 'Twas no use, though. He found out about it and clapped us all in jail. We are waiting now, to be burnt at sunrise."

"Why, so are we!" said Ann.

"Practically everybody is," said De Bracy, gloomily.

"Where's Rowena?" Ann wondered. "You seemed to be awfully good friends the last time I saw you."

The Norman's face darkened. "Never speak that

name," he said. " 'Twas she who betrayed me. She maketh her great eyes at the Leader now. She hopeth to be Leaderess. When the guards arrested me, she laughed."

"I'm not a bit surprised," said Ann. "She never was good enough even for you, let alone Ivanhoe. I always kind of liked you. For a villain, you weren't bad at all."

"Thanks," said De Bracy, blushing modestly. "Then perhaps in that case thou wouldst not mind rescuing me and my comrades? I have heard tell that thou art a mighty sorceress."

"Oh," said Ann, blushing now in her turn. "Well, about that." Then she broke off, staring at his luxurious curling blond whiskers. She had almost forgotten about the quest. Now she remembered. "All right," she said. "But first there's just one thing."

"Anything, anything," said De Bracy.

"First," said Ann, "I'll have to cut off your beard."

"What?" The Norman's hand flew up to cover his beautiful whiskers protectively. He stood glaring at her in mistrust.

"I need it," said Ann, "for my mighty sorcery. Besides, it will soon grow out again," she added, feeling sorry for his knightly dignity.

"Well," said De Bracy reluctantly, offering her his sword, "see that thou cuttest clean and pullest not the short hairs." And he laid his head trustfully down on the stone windowsill.

One clean sweep, and the beard was in Ann's hands. She put it carefully with the roses, and checked off another item in her notebook. For the beard was what she had made of the small giant's side-curls one day when she decided De Bracy's face needed an extra touch. Now if she could just remember about the coattails.

"Well?" said De Bracy, when a minute had gone by and nothing had happened. "When doth the mighty sorcery begin?"

"Wait," said Ann, playing for time. "I can't do it all alone. I have to wait for Roger and the witch."

Another minute passed.

"When will they be coming?" said De Bracy.

"Pretty soon," said Ann. "I hope."

"Where are they now?" said De Bracy.

Ann couldn't keep up the pretense any longer. Her lip trembled. "I wish I knew," she said.

While all this was happening, Roger and Eliza were steadily trudging over the plain toward the forest. When they came to the shrubbery at the edge of the wood, Eliza stopped and picked a few leaves.

"Here," she said, handing them to Roger. "The giants' bath mat."

And they were in Sherwood itself. But the mighty forest seemed different today. No birds sang in its trees, no deer galloped gaily down its corridors. Even Eliza's bright conversation dwindled. Suddenly she grabbed Roger's arm. "Chiggers!" she said.

Roger stopped short. Someone was watching them, from behind a tree just ahead. It was a man in Lincoln green, but his jerkin was frayed and worn and his hose had holes in the knees. He had a bow in his hand, but he seemed to lack the strength to use it. He was staring at them with cold, unfriendly eyes that burned in a face so thin and worn that they didn't recognize him at first. Then they did, and ran to him with joyful cries of "Robin!"

But Robin Hood made an effort and raised his bow threateningly. "Stop where ye are, false prophets!" he cried. "Ye have tricked us with lies and led us astray that the vile Prince—I will not call him Leader for he certainly leadeth not *me*—might pillage our noble greenwood and rob us of our livelihood!"

"No we didn't. Honest," said Roger.

"We were unavoidably detained," said Eliza.

"We couldn't help it. It was magic. It does that sometimes," said Roger.

At last Robin Hood was convinced. "Then thank

Heaven ye have returned," he said. "It hath been horrible."

And he raised his horn and blew a faint but cheered-up blast, and the rest of the outlaws came out of their woodsy hiding, but so changed and weary that Roger would not have known them, and with many missing from their ranks.

Then as they sat on the ground, Robin told Roger and Eliza what De Bracy had told Ann, all about how Prince John was Leader now. And he told them how Prince John had rounded up all the deer in the forest for a collective farming experiment, so that the merry men were reduced to living on berries and tree bark. And how afterwards when they were weakened he had hunted them down with his terrible new army.

Many had been wounded and many more had deserted and fled. But the best men of the band were still loyally hoping for Roger and Ivanhoe to return and lead them to crush Prince John forever.

"Had I my trusty sword by me I shouldst have done it long ago," said the Black Knight. "Where is it?"

"Goodness," said Roger. "It must be in the Giants' Lair, still!" And he and Eliza told them about their adventure with the giants (leaving out the parts that were too magic for them to understand).

"And the mighty Jack?" said Robin Hood, "and the small sorceress?"

Eliza told about their quest, and how Ann and Jack must be somewhere in Torquilstone Castle this very minute.

"Then woe betide them!" cried Maid Marian. "The Prince hath taken it, and is burning folk at sunrise right and left!"

At this, Roger wanted to turn back and rescue Ann right away, but the others dissuaded him. "They've probably found everything and got away by this time," said Eliza. "They're probably on their way here right now. They'll probably be turning up any minute."

"Besides," said Robin Hood, "my men are in no condition to attack." So it was decided that Robin and the Black Knight should ride with Roger and Eliza to the Giants' Lair, while the others rested and consumed what rations they had, in preparation for battle.

"I hate to do this," said Eliza, after she had explained to Cedric the Saxon about needing his cloak for the quest. "Won't you be cold?"

"If 'twill aid my son," said Cedric, "what matter if back and side go bare?" And Friar Tuck said he'd lend him his extra habit, anyway.

The journey to the Lair passed quickly, and

Robin and the Black Knight waited at the edge of the wood while Roger and Eliza hurried across the giants' lawn. And the door stood open for Eliza, and the three smiling giants appeared in it.

They were more civil than they had been before, and thanked the children for the return of the furniture. The mother giant was a bit sniffy about the worn condition of Cedric's cloak, but when she put the velvet next to her gown it attached itself and suddenly looked as good as new. And the bits of fur grew back into the fur coat beautifully.

The bath mat, alas, was never quite the same, and looked more like a group of leaves than a bath mat for the rest of its life, but the female giant actually smiled and said she liked it better that way. "Quite artistic."

Eliza then asked to see the prisoners, and sure enough, Ivanhoe still had his bandage on under his armor, and though it now made rather a mussy pair of kitchen curtains, the giant family agreed that it would be quite a souvenir.

As for the rest of the things, Roger explained that his sister was bringing those, but had been delayed. "Couldn't you trust us?" he asked. "Couldn't you let our friends go now, sort of on credit?" And Eliza joined her voice to his, assuring the giants that they would have their other belongings back soon.

"Why not?" said the mother giant. "I have heard of getting things on the installment plan, and this must be what it means."

"Well," said the father giant, "I pride myself on being a fair giant. Two may leave, but one must stay as hostage."

"Allow me," said Bois-Guilbert, nobly. "Let the best man win. The extra wait will give me more time to repent, anyway."

"Thanks a lot, old man," said Roger, before Ivanhoe could start being self-sacrificing, too. "That's darn nice of you."

And he and Eliza grabbed Ivanhoe and Rebecca and ran out of the house and across the lawn with them, to where Robin Hood and the Black Knight waited. And the giant let them take the Black Knight's sword with them, just to show what a fair giant he really was.

Once the Black Knight found its hilt in his hand again he declared himself ready to tame a thousand Saracens, let alone one measly Leader, who was only his little brother, anyway! And Robin Hood started looking less thin and worn, already.

When they reached the clearing all was excitement, as the outlaws prepared horses and weapons for the coming battle. Roger noticed a silver-bearded figure busying itself in the thick of the activity. He thought he knew who the silver-bearded one was, but every time he tried to get near him to make sure, the bearded one was suddenly somewhere else.

But each place he had been, the horses suddenly looked sturdier and the weapons sharper and keener and the merry men stronger and merrier, till at last, when Robin wound his horn in the signal for departure, it was a lusty and mettlesome battalion that set out for Torquilstone. No one would have known them for the starving outcasts they had been a few hours before.

Eliza rode by the side of Roger. "Don't look now," she said, after a few minutes, "but hark behind you."

Roger harked. "Father," Ivanhoe was saying to Cedric the Saxon, "this may make thee very angry, but my troth is plighted to Rebecca. I can never marry the Lady Rowena now."

"Son," said Cedric, "it doth not make me angry one whit. Thy Rebecca is a maid of courage and honor, and bonny besides. As for the Lady Rowena, she hath proved herself a false jade. I say down with her."

"So *that's* all right," said Eliza.

Yes, thought Roger to himself, things were looking up. Hope sang high in his heart as he galloped toward Torquilstone.

Meanwhile, in the dungeon, Maurice De Bracy was getting restless. "Really!" he said to Ann, crossly. "Half the day hath passed now, and no sorcery!"

"I know," said Ann, unhappily. "I'm sorry."

"So far as I can see, cutting off my beard hath not done one speck of good. Canst thou not at least put it back on again?"

"No," said Ann. "I can't."

"Humph!" said De Bracy. "Thy magic seemeth pretty small pumpkins to me."

Jack was standing by one of the barred windows, looking out. "That's what *you* think," he said, suddenly.

There was a confused noise from outside, and a sound of running feet. Then voices began to shout, and their words sent a thrill through each prisoner's heart. "To arms!" said the voices. "The enemy is attacking!"

Jack grinned at Ann. "You see?" he said to De Bracy triumphantly.

De Bracy went down on one knee before Ann. "I take it back," he said. "Hail, mighty sorceress!"

"Don't mention it," said Ann.

At that moment bolts were shot back, keys turned in locks, and the great dungeon door swung wide. A man appeared in the doorway. He wore a silver beard, and if Roger had seen him, he'd have wondered how he got here so quickly from Robin Hood's camp.

The bearded one said nothing, and nothing needed to be said. With one accord the prisoners streamed out of the dungeon to freedom, and as they passed, the bearded one handed each a weapon from a seemingly endless store he had with him. Ann and Jack came last.

"Hello," said Ann. "You're awfully helpful all of a sudden. Does that mean it's a good sign?"

The Old One said nothing, but he winked at Ann before he disappeared.

"Come on!" said Jack. And he and Ann raced out of the dungeon. Then they flattened themselves against the side of the building just in time. For Prince John himself appeared right in front of them, riding by at the head of his army.

"Follow your Leader!" he was shouting as he rode past. "We are twice their strength and have better weapons besides! Wait till we have them in our power! *Then* heads will roll!"

He and his army dashed out the castle gates,

and Ann turned to Jack. "Let's get somewhere where we can see!"

Of course Jack yearned to be in the battle, but he didn't think he should leave Ann unprotected. "Let's try the roof," he said. "Maybe we can help from there." So they ran through the courtyard and up the stairway to the battlements.

The varlet Hugo was already there, tending some cauldrons of molten lead, as usual. Jack took him by surprise and threw him over the edge, and his molten lead after him. Then he dusted his hands and turned to photographing the scene below.

Ann looked and caught her breath. The armies were spread out beneath, like a bright-colored moving tapestry. Trumpets sounded, and flights of arrows soared like fireworks. Then the front lines crashed together, like two great waves meeting in a storm. And Prince John's men *were* stronger, and the line of Lincoln green wavered and fell back, and Ann shut her eyes.

But Prince John had reckoned without De Bracy and the other escaped prisoners, who now came charging onto the field and attacked him from the rear. Caught between two fires, the Prince's men hesitated, and in the pause Robin's forces rallied and came at them with renewed vigor.

When Ann cautiously opened her eyes and looked again, the two armies were tangled in a free-for-all, and none could say who was winning, but anyone could see Prince John was hard pressed.

And now the tide of battle swung nearer the castle, and Ann and Jack gasped. There, riding the crest of it, was Eliza. She had borrowed a helmet and shield from somebody, and was laughing and whacking about her like some wild battle goddess, her boastful cries ringing on the air.

And there, just behind Eliza, Ann saw Roger. He wasn't laughing but he was fighting just as hard. The next minute another turn of the tide swept them both out of sight.

But now Prince John seemed to feel that enough was enough. He and his men turned tail and cut their way back through De Bracy's followers till they gained the castle. Ann and Jack were afraid they might try to defend it, and find them on the roof, but the Prince and his men merely packed up their goods and chattels, and did a few other things, before escaping by a back door, just as the triumphant merry men rode up to the front one, to claim Torquilstone for Richard Lionheart.

And Ann and Jack went running down from the parapet to be the first to offer their congratulations.

"Oh, good, you're still alive," said Eliza, galloping up beside Roger, as the victorious army surged toward the castle. "I cut off four heads and cleaved three knights in two. How did you do?"

"All right, I guess," said Roger. Actually he had fought with valor and joined in several quite good deadly combats. But battles, he decided, were more fun when they were pretend ones than when they were real, even magically real. He had seen his duty and he had done it, but he didn't want to talk about it.

There was a slight delay at Torquilstone, for Prince John had left the drawbridge up. But Robin Hood gallantly swam the moat and forced his way into the guardtower and let down the bridge.

And at that moment the portcullis went up, and Ann and Jack appeared in the opening.

"Hi," said Jack to Robin Hood. "Come on in. The battle was fine."

And the gallant army trooped over the bridge, and the four cousins were reunited, and the voice of Eliza rang loud on the courtyard air, as she boasted of her prowess upon the field.

In the castle keep Rowena came smiling up to them, carrying a banner she had hastily embroidered that said, "Victory!" She tried to fling herself into Ivanhoe's arms, but Rebecca was already there, and repulsed her. So then she came swarming up to Robin Hood and Roger, but to no avail. She was roundly snubbed by everybody.

"Traitress," said King Richard, "we have heard of thy faithless dealings. Thou art under arrest. Away with her."

Rowena was hustled away to the dungeon.

"And now," said King Richard, "what say ye

all to a feast to celebrate our victory and refresh our war-weary limbs?" And all the weary warriors cheered.

"Only no roast venison, please," said Eliza.

"Is this the happy ending?" Ann whispered to Roger, as several dozen minions scurried away to the kitchen. "Have you earned the wish already, do you suppose?"

"It seems as if," said Roger, "but I don't see how it can be. I haven't done a thing yet, really. And what about the ancient rune?"

"That's right," said Ann. "I forgot."

"I didn't," said Roger. "I've been thinking about it all the time."

"Let's think some more," said Ann. And she got her notebook out and studied it.

Maurice De Bracy, who had been looking unhappy ever since Rowena was hustled away, now stepped forward and started to kneel before the king and say something. But before he could, there was an interruption.

The minions who had been sent to prepare the feast came running back into the room, all talking at once and wringing their hands and saying, "Wurra wurra." When King Richard finally got sense out of them, it turned out that before Prince John's men left the castle, they had thrown away or poisoned every bit of food in the kitchens, and there wasn't a smidgin left to have a small meal with, let alone a feast.

And just as this blow was sinking in, Little John, who had been left in charge of the guard at the gates, came hurrying in with a face of doom. "'Tis that Prince John," he cried. "He be back with more army than before! He hath surrounded us! The park and the castle we still hold, but that be all!"

Everyone went running to look. It was true. Beyond the park and all around the castle on every side stretched a ring of armed men.

"'Tis a blockade! He meaneth to starve us out!" cried Robin Hood.

"You see?" said Roger to Ann.

"What a scurvy trick! If that be not just like him!" said King Richard. "But he hath not won the game yet! Robin, call your men. Ivanhoe, follow me! We shall carve our way out!"

"My men couldn't stand it," said Robin Hood. "Not on an empty stomach. I couldn't, either."

"Nor I," said Ivanhoe. "And speak not of carving, for thou makest my mouth water."

"Hm," said King Richard. "Now that thou mentionest it, I feel very much the same." He turned to Roger. "Methinks there be only one among us who can help us now."

"Who, me?" said Roger.

King Richard nodded solemnly. "What is thy Elfish counsel? What shall we do?"

Roger gulped. He looked at King Richard and Robin Hood and Ivanhoe and they looked back at him with appeal in their eyes, and he didn't have a thought in his head.

"Wait a minute," he said. "Maybe I'll think of something."

Everybody waited.

Ann had heard all this, but only with part of her mind. The other part was still thinking about the ancient rune. Her eyes went from her notebook to the park with the statue of St. George Peabody, and back to her notebook again. And an idea started forming in her mind.

She thought of something, and then she thought of something else. And then she knew what she had to do. She supposed she ought to tell Roger and let *him* do it, but he was busy just now.

The only thing was, she would have to go away for a little while to do it, and she didn't want her going to disturb any of the others. Maybe if she left quietly, no one would notice. Maybe she could even slip away alone and come back again without anyone's knowing she had been gone.

So, not using her voice at all, but just saying them in her mind, Ann thought two words. I leave you to imagine what words they were.

But it seemed that Words of Power are Words of Power whether you speak them out loud or not. For the mist came down and the castle disappeared, and the next minute Ann was back in Roger's room, and Eliza and Jack were standing glaring at her with expressions of utter exasperation.

"What in the world did you do that for?" said Jack.

"Just when it was getting interesting, too!" said Eliza.

Ann paid them no heed. "I worked it out! I worked out the ancient rune!" she cried, turning to tell Roger.

Then she broke off. Roger wasn't there.

8

The Ending

"Where is he?" said Ann, stupidly, gazing at where Roger should have been.

"*I* don't know," said Jack, looking around the room. "I hardly know where I am myself, yet."

"We must have left him behind," said Eliza. "He must be back there in the magic, still."

"And now we'll have to wait three days before we find out," said Jack.

"Oh dear," Ann wailed. "I thought I could just get away and back by myself, but if you're here, too, then it's over, just like the other times. Only if that's true, why didn't he come along? He always got home all right before. Last time, and the Flying Saucer time, and that first time when we weren't with him!"

She broke off and her face paled, as a horrid possibility dawned. "Oh dear," she said. "Magic goeth by threes."

"You mean the words only work three times for each one, and now he's had his, and he's *stuck* there?" said Eliza. *"Forever?"*

Jack nodded solemnly. "It stands to reason."

A worse thought occurred to Eliza. "And now you've made me use my third time, and if we go back again to get him I'll be stuck, too, and so will you!"

Ann set her chin stubbornly. "Maybe we won't," she said. "Maybe now I know the rune it'll be all different."

"What rune?" said Eliza.

"The ancient rune," said Ann.

"You mean you've guessed it?" said Jack.

"Yes, but I haven't time to talk about it now," said Ann. "I have to do something."

She reached down and picked the Old One up,

from the castle. "Oh Old One," she said, "you needn't answer, and don't bother warming up if it's any trouble, but please couldn't you not count this time and let us go back as soon as I've finished? I know what the rune means now. Wait and see."

She put the Old One back in the castle and ran out of the room. Her feet were heard clattering on the stairs.

"Where's she going?" said Jack. He and Eliza ran into the hall and hung over the stairwell.

From below came a sound of drawers opening and shutting, and a clatter of cutlery.

"She's in the kitchen," said Jack. "What's she doing?"

"She's crazy," said Eliza. "It's all been too much for her and her mind's given way."

Ann came running back up the stairs, an intent expression on her face and something in her hand. She hurried past Jack and Eliza without a word, and into Roger's room.

"What was that in her hand?" said Eliza.

"It looked like a can-opener," said Jack.

"It couldn't be," said Eliza.

They followed Ann into the room. Ann went over to the castle and did something. Then she went to Roger's bureau. There was a big tied-up box on top of the bureau, and she undid the string and opened the lid. So far as Jack and Eliza could see, there was nothing in the box but a lot of cotton.

"There," said Ann. "Now we can go. At least I hope we can." She looked over toward where the Old One was, in the castle. "Did I guess right? Can we go now? Please?"

"You mean you interrupted everything and spoiled it all just to come back and do *that*?" said Jack.

"I told you," said Eliza. "The girl's balmy. Stark, raving daft!" But she was wrong.

And Ann paid her words no heed. "Look!" she said, pointing to the walls of the room.

Jack and Eliza looked where she pointed. There weren't any walls. And the gray mist came swirling, and it was just like the other times, only backwards, because the next moment they were standing in the park before Torquilstone Castle, and Ivanhoe and Rebecca and Robin Hood and King Richard and a whole crowd of others were standing there, too, and everybody was cheering.

The children looked to see what all the shouting was for. And then they knew.

Roger was staring at the floor, trying desperately to think of a way out, when he heard Ann utter the Words of Power.

For though Ann merely thought them, the words

were so powerful that the sound of them rang and echoed through the room, and everyone heard.

And despair filled the heart of Roger.

This was the end. And now Ann had given up and deserted, and she was probably perfectly right to, and something told Roger this was his last chance, and he'd never earn his wish now.

He waited for the gray mist to carry him away, but it didn't. What he saw now was what Ivanhoe and Rebecca and Bois-Guilbert and the giants had seen on other occasions, and if Roger hadn't been beyond all caring, it would have been interesting to watch.

For a bright cloud descended and enveloped Ann and Jack and Eliza and sailed away with them, and left Roger standing right where he was.

And then he, too, remembered about magic going by threes, and he felt even worse. Not only had he failed, but he was lost here in this magic world forever! And he knew it was only what he deserved.

"Thy friends have gone," said King Richard, after a moment. "I presume thou hast sent them on some magic errand to save us?"

"No," said Roger, "I didn't. I wish I had. I would have if I could have thought of any."

"Can it be," said the king, "that they have fled?" And a frown of anger clouded his brow.

"I guess that's what they've done," said Roger, looking at his feet.

"But then surely we must despair," cried the king, paling, "if magic itself giveth us up as hopeless!"

"Yes," said Roger. "I guess you might as well. I'm sorry. It's all my fault."

"Dost mean that thou hast betrayed us on *purpose*?" cried King Richard, outraged. "Is thy magic *black*?"

"Not exactly," said Roger, "but it might as well be. I'm just plain no good at it. I don't have the touch. I thought I did, but I don't. And you don't know the worst part."

The worst part, of course, was about his father, but he couldn't talk about that. He could only think about it, and he did.

But it was then, in Roger's darkest hour, that help came.

Little John, who had gone to check with the guard, came running back in again.

"A miracle, sire!" he cried. "Help from the skies!"

More guards came running in after him, shouting. "The sword! The sword!" cried some. And others cried, "The statue!"

Everyone ran into the park. Sure enough, from

the statue of St. George Peabody a great sword protruded. It hung at a peculiar angle, as though someone had stuck it in at the top, and then levered it down to one side.

"Behold," said Little John, "a great hand hath appeared from above, and placed it there!"

"Many have tried, but none can pull it forth," cried those who were nearest the statue, and had been trying.

"What can it mean?" everybody was saying.

But Roger had remembered the ancient rune, and he knew what it meant. At least he thought he did. And his heart gave a great leap.

And like the young King Arthur before him, he stepped up to the sword, and took it by the hilt, and it came away easily in his hands. He looked up, and there was the Old One, standing beside him smiling at him. And for the first time in all the magic adventures, the Old One spoke.

"Sword from stone the hero taketh," he said.

And then a great cheer went up from the whole multitude. For out of the cloven statue gushed a stream of rich liquid and a delicious aroma pervaded the air. And all the hungry people came with ramekins and pannikins and bowls, and drank from that fount of plenty. And a cloud of glory descended from the sky and brought Ann and Jack and Eliza with it, and Roger saw Ann smiling at him, and he realized what it was that she had done.

"Have some soup," he said, and Ann knew that in those words he was saying all the things that nobody can ever say, particularly when he is a boy talking to his little sister.

And she and Roger and Eliza and Jack agreed afterwards that it was the best pea soup they ever tasted.

It seemed to have other properties, too—added vitamins, maybe. For as its rich warmth coursed through their veins, all the knights and yeomen felt suddenly refreshed and strong again, and couldn't wait to fall upon the army of the dastard Prince.

"Follow me, Ivanhoe's men!" cried Wilfred, and Robin Hood blew his hunting horn, and all their loyal band gathered round them.

"Wait," called a voice. It was the Old One. He pointed. "The Snowbound Sleepers!"

Everyone looked.

Far in the distance whitely gleamed a snow-capped mountain nobody remembered ever having seen before. And all the people cried out, "More miracles!"

For strains of martial music were heard from the mountain, and down its side marched a company of such soldiers as the eyes of chivalry had never yet gazed upon.

"Wow!" said Jack. "The U.S. Marines to the rescue!"

"Well, sort of," said Ann, modestly.

As Eliza said later, it was like a Memorial Day parade. There were British grenadiers singing *The British Grenadiers*, and modern G.I.'s singing *The Beer Barrel Polka*, and 1918 doughboys singing *Over There*! And last and most impressive of all, marched the Spanish War veterans. "Remember the Maine!" they cried. "Remember Teddy Roosevelt! Charge!"

And the men of Prince John gave way and scattered before them and they kept on marching straight up to the castle.

Roger looked at them with love and pride, and realized that only he knew the record and capabilities of each and every one of them, and only he was fitted to be their general. Brandishing the sword he had pulled from the stone, he took his place at their head, and Jack and Robin Hood and King Richard and Ivanhoe fell into line just behind him, and the merry men followed after.

But when they saw the whites of the enemy's eyes, and Roger waved his sword in the command to fire, and when the Prince's soldiers heard gunpowder for the first time, they fell on their knees holding their ears in craven surrender, and Prince John fled all by himself.

And they hunted him over hill, over dale, through bush and through brier, till in the end he took refuge in Sherwood Forest, which was foolish of him, because Robin Hood knew every tree and every inch of it, and they found the wretched Prince at last, cowering behind a bush, alone and miserable and Leader of nobody. And they marched him back a prisoner to Torquilstone.

His judgment was pronounced by King Richard that very day, in the castle keep. All were present. Prince John made a contemptible picture, as he sniveled in the prisoner's dock.

"Come, come," said King Richard. "Crying will get thee nowhere. Thou wert ever the same, e'en when we were boys together. Nothing but a pest!"

"To the block with him!" called somebody.

"Melt him down," called somebody else, "in his own molten lead!"

"Nay," said the king. "I cannot slay my own brother, richly though he deserve it. Go forth," he said to Prince John, "to lead a hermit's life alone in the wilderness, bereft of thy title, and let all men shun thee forever."

And Prince John slunk away.

"But won't he come back and make more trouble

later?" whispered Ann, who was seated on the king's left. "Later on in history?"

King Richard shook his head. "History no longer hath meaning for us now. And what is even better, after this no more terrible ideas from the world outside can penetrate here. Time standeth still from now on, and the golden age of chivalry endureth forever, now that the hero"—and here he nodded at Roger, who was seated upon his right hand—"hath set us free."

Roger started to protest at this, but now Maurice De Bracy stepped forward and knelt before the king.

"Sire," he said, "I started to say this before, but there was an interruption. I have been thy enemy in the past, but I have repented. I crave pardon and shall do any penance thou wishest."

"De Bracy," said Richard, "thou wert ever an honorable foe, and thou hast fought valiantly in the recent battles. I pardon thee."

"I crave another boon," said De Bracy. "If it please thee, set free the Lady Rowena, who now languisheth in durance vile. Traitress or not, I love her and would have her for my bride."

"Oh, very well," said King Richard, "though sooner you than me. Take her far from here and let living with her be thy penance."

And Rowena was brought from the dungeon and

fell into De Bracy's arms. So *that* was all right.
There was still the quest unfinished, but Ivanhoe

and Rebecca volunteered to stop off and deliver the
final installment at the Giants' Lair, on their wed-

ding journey. And at last Ann remembered what she had done with the father giant's coattails.

She hadn't done anything with them. She had cut them off, and then forgotten about them, and put them down somewhere. They finally turned up in the scullery, where the kitchenmaid had cut them up for dishcloths. King Richard had them laundered, and Rebecca tied them up in a neat package with De Bracy's beard and the roses, which were sadly wilted by now.

And then the four children said a fond good-bye to Ivanhoe and Rebecca, who were anxious to depart on their honeymoon.

"Now we'll never know what finally became of Bois-Guilbert," said Ann.

"He's probably so reformed by now he probably won't be fit for normal life," said Eliza. "He'll probably go enter a monastery." And I believe that is probably exactly what he did.

Roger was getting anxious to depart now, too, for something told him it was time. But King Richard said he couldn't possibly leave till he and Robin Hood gave a banquet in his honor. And in spite of all that Roger could, and did, say, they gave it for him that night.

And after the banquet everyone drank to Roger,

and then came a cry of "Speech! Speech!" from the whole company, and Roger stood up and faced them all.

"Thanks a lot," he said, "and I just want to say I don't deserve any of it. I haven't been a hero a bit. The first time I came there wouldn't have been any trouble if I hadn't started it by talking too much. And the next two times I wasn't a speck of help to hardly anybody. And this last time there wouldn't have been any sword in the stone, or any army for me to be general of, if Ann hadn't worked out the secret rune when I couldn't, and she did just about the whole thing, and if there's any toasts going to be drunk, they ought to be to her. And I drink to her now."

And he drained his glass, and then smashed it on the stone floor, and sat down and blushed and didn't look at anybody, though Ann was looking at him and smiling for all she was worth.

But to his surprise the cheers now were louder than they had been before, and Robin Hood cried that that was the most heroic speech he ever did hear, pardie! And the Old One came all the way around the table and shook Roger's hand.

"Wisdom now the hero learneth," he said.

Roger looked at him. "You mean?"

"Wait," said the Old One. And he turned to the others. "Three cheers for Roger," he cried, "and may his name live forever, for the way he hath led soldiers!"

"He led soldiers! Led soldiers! Led soldiers!" cheered the whole company, and these were the most beautiful Words of Power (or of anything else) that Roger had ever heard in his life.

And the gray mist came down for the last time, and wafted the four children away in its soft nothingness, and the next Roger knew he was lying in bed and it was a bright morning of sun and blue sky, and his mother was standing over him with such a smile on her face that Roger knew he must have earned his wish at last, and it had come true.

Later that day he learned how his father had come through better than anyone had expected, and he was going to be fine. In fact, he was going to be better so soon that he could leave the hospital in just a little while now, and they were going to spend the rest of the summer on an island in a lake in the mountains on the boundary between New England and Canada, because that was the nearest they could get to the four different vacations the family had wanted.

"Though after the magic," said Eliza, when the

four children were alone, "even the desertest island would seem paltry."

"I don't know," said Roger. "I'll be kind of glad to get back to normal. Not that it wasn't wonderful," he added quickly. "At least most of it was."

"And now we'll never see them again," said Jack. "I'm going to miss that Robin Hood. Those were the days."

"We can still play with them," said Ann. "I think they'll kind of *know*."

"I never did get my special adventure," said Eliza. "It turned out to be somebody else's every time."

"Maybe that was on purpose," said Jack, grinning at her. "Maybe that was just to teach you."

Eliza looked surprised. Then slowly a smile spread over her face. "Well, for Heaven's sake," she said. "If that wouldn't be just like that magic's impudence! Trying to teach *me* moral lessons! Maybe you're right, though," she added, seriously. Maybe that's why it came into our lives, to make noble characters of us. I learned not to be bossy, and Ann learned to be brave and think for herself."

"And I learned there ackcherly is magic," said Jack.

"And I learned wisdom," said Roger, looking so smug and holy that Jack and Eliza fell on him and held him down and sat on him while Ann tickled his feet till he admitted that maybe he did have a *little* more to learn, still.

"I wish I could give you a picture to remember it all by," said Jack, when peace reigned again. "I had a keen one of you leading the army, but it didn't come out. None of them did."

"I didn't think they would, somehow," said Ann.

"I wonder if we'll ever have another summer together," said Roger.

"I wonder if it'll be a magic one," said Jack.

"Wottest thou not that all magic goeth by threes?" said Eliza. "Maybe we'll have two more!"

"Time will tell," said Ann.

And it did.

Edward Eager (1911–1964) worked primarily as a playwright and lyricist. It wasn't until 1951, while searching for books to read to his young son, Fritz, that he began writing children's stories. In each of his books he carefully acknowledges his indebtedness to E. Nesbit, whom he considered the best children's writer of all time—"so that any child who likes my books and doesn't know hers may be led back to the master of us all."